"I want you to marry me."

"No!" Cynthia said sharply, then, "Why? We've hardly spoken to each other in years! This has to be a joke."

Jonathan stood, and placed his hands flat on the counter. "It's not a joke. Call it a gamble if you like."

"What do you get out of it? What do you want?" Her voice turned brittle.

"You can be sure it's not your money—"

"Then *why*?"

He leaned forward. "I want you."

Vanessa Grant began writing her first romance when she was twelve years old. The novel foundered on page fifty, but Vanessa never forgot the magic of having a love story come to life. Although she went on to become an accountant and a college instructor, she never stopped writing and, in 1985, her first Harlequin® novel was published. Vanessa and her husband live in a log home in the forest on one of British Columbia's Gulf Islands.

The Moon Lady's Lover
Vanessa Grant

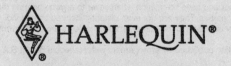

TORONTO • NEW YORK • LONDON
AMSTERDAM • PARIS • SYDNEY • HAMBURG
STOCKHOLM • ATHENS • TOKYO • MILAN • MADRID
PRAGUE • WARSAW • BUDAPEST • AUCKLAND

For Nicholas James Wallace on the occasion of his birth

ISBN 0-373-17398-9

THE MOON LADY'S LOVER

First North American Publication 1998.

This edition published by arrangement with Harlequin Books S.A.

® and TM are trademarks of the publisher. Trademarks indicated with
® are registered in the United States Patent and Trademark Office, the
Canadian Trade Marks Office and in other countries.

Printed in U.S.A.

CHAPTER ONE

WHEN the jet landed in Vancouver, Cynthia Dyson-Paige was still rehearsing what she would say to Jonathan Halley. She'd been practising the words all through the four-hour flight from Toronto.

She rented a car at the airport, wincing as her credit card went through the imprinting machine. Then she crawled into Vancouver with the morning rush-hour traffic, still rehearsing the encounter to come.

I thought you'd want to help Allan. He needs help. . .

She tried to hear Jonathan's response in her mind but that part of the conversation was a blank. She knew it was outrageous that she should come to him like this, ridiculous to think that she could ask him for help when they hadn't spoken a civil word in the fourteen years since she was sixteen.

There were no other options.

I came to ask you for money. . .

Since yesterday she'd spent hours fantasising how it would be. He wouldn't smile when he saw her. She hadn't called to say she was coming, so he wouldn't be expecting her. He'd look up from his desk in that high-rise building in Vancouver's financial district and both his mouth and his eyes would frown.

Three months ago she'd seen pictures in a magazine article and she knew the décor of his office, even the scope of the ocean view out of the window. So when she said silently, Jonathan, I need help, her mind instantly provided the surroundings from the magazine pictures.

It hadn't occurred to her that he wouldn't be there, but at nine-thirty she was thirteen storeys above the ground listening to a well-groomed female dragon tell her that Mr Halley was out of town.

'Where is he?' If he was in Toronto it would be ironic because she'd just flown across the continent searching for him. But better Toronto than Europe because she might not be able to get an immediate overseas flight.

She couldn't afford to waste a day.

The dragon frowned under iron-tidy hair but it seemed that Jonathan's movements weren't secret because she said, 'On Vancouver Island. A little village called Parkland.'

Oh, God. . .

When her father's estate was wound up Cynthia had seen Jonathan's name on the Agreement for Sale for the Parkland estate. She hadn't known why he had bought it but she was never going back there so it hardly mattered. Then last winter she'd read that Jonathan Halley was part of a consortium building a luxury hotel on inner Vancouver Island and she'd known that there would be concrete forms and bull-dozers standing squarely on land that had once belonged to her father.

Jonathan. . .

It was the last place she would choose to face him again.

It took three more hours to get there. Across to Vancouver Island by ferry, then north to Parkland. She stopped at a motel just outside the village. The beaches were full of holiday-makers but sunshine and whitecaps were lost on her. The desk clerk pushed her credit card through the imprinting machine and she felt the now familiar wave of nausea, but her financial mess was so deep that one more credit card charge hardly mattered.

In her room she showered and changed into a harvest-gold suit with matching pumps. She added a pearl necklace with matching earrings and brushed her hair to glossy submission. She frowned at the mirror until she had the waist-length chestnut strands gathered into a smooth knot at the back of her neck and anchored with a clasp that matched the necklace.

Subdued lipstick. Matching nail polish. Colour co-ordinated. Jonathan wouldn't give a damn, but she wasn't about to face him in anything less than full armour. Cynthia Dyson-Paige might be the only person living in all North America who didn't like Jonathan Halley, but at least she had the satisfaction of knowing it was mutual.

She was as ready as she would ever be.

Rural Parkland. Small. Quiet. From what she could see of the construction site, Jonathan was doing his best to change that.

She'd spent half her childhood here, but the old manor house was gone now. So were most of the woods where she'd played hide-and-seek with Allan — cut down for Jonathan's new hotel.

Jonathan. . .even in those days she'd watched him laugh and charm and plan his way to his goals — but it was years since he'd had a smile for her.

She stopped when she saw the sign. Jonathan's name printed there as architect, a stylised picture of the resort as it might look when it was finished in a year's time. The developer's name in larger letters — a holding company that she knew Jonathan controlled. Off to the right was a yellow and white trailer with three trucks parked outside it.

That was where she would find him. She took a deep breath and went up the three steps to the door of the trailer.

She had flown three thousand miles to see him and she dreaded it. It was a year since the last time she'd caught his black eyes across a crowded room. Five years since she'd exchanged words with him. They hadn't been friendly words.

His smile would die the instant he saw her.

She was surrounded by the organised chaos of concrete forms and machinery. Off to the right the land fell away and the ocean gave an incongruous slash of blue through the branches of an old apple tree. She tightened her grip on the doorknob of the trailer. He'd left *that* tree standing.

This was *his* project. His design and his money behind it.

She had to focus on the money. She wasn't here because of the past. She'd come because Jonathan Halley could lay his hands on a lot of money fast.

She heard laughter from inside the construction trailer.

Jonathan's laughter.

She turned the knob and pushed the door open. Inside, the trailer was filled with coffee and blueprints and muscular men who looked to Jonathan for answers. They were gathered around him; tough men caught in a moment of relaxation. Jonathan's lanky form was sitting casually on the edge of a desk.

She remembered the last words he'd said to her.

Five years ago. Toronto. Her father's funeral. He was the last person she'd expected to see. 'What are you doing here?' she'd demanded.

'Making sure.'

'Making sure he's dead?' she'd gasped. Jonathan and her father had hated each other but she wouldn't have thought Jonathan capable of making such a cruel comment on the day of her father's funeral. 'How could you?' she'd whispered, staring at him.

Black suit. . .black hair. . .black eyes. Unsmiling face.

'Perhaps I'm checking up on *you*,' he'd said.

'I'm married,' she'd retorted. His eyes had flared and she'd had to fight the urge to jerk back from him.

'Of course you are,' he'd agreed in a grim voice. 'But I wouldn't count on Eric McAulisson if I were you. Call me, moon lady, when you've got trouble.'

As if he expected her to have trouble. . .to turn to *him* for help.

'You're the last person I'd call!' she'd hissed. 'I'd roast in hell first!'

If anyone in her life could be called her enemy it was Jonathan Halley. And it was mutual because, when she stepped into that construction trailer and all the men turned to look at her, Jonathan was the one who didn't smile. The echo of relaxed camaraderie was still lurking among the blueprints but his black eyes turned cold when they saw her.

A husky man wearing an orange hard-hat breathed, 'He-ello there!' He was the oldest of the workers and he wore an air of command. He put down his coffee-cup, confident and capable and moving towards the counter to stake his claim on this city-dressed stranger. 'What can I do for you, ma'am?'

Jonathan said quietly, 'Cynthia.' Just her name, not a greeting.

The older man backed off immediately. 'We'll get back to it, then,' he said and they all began to move towards the door.

Except Jonathan.

'I want to see that east wall before you pour,' he said, his eyes holding Cynthia's.

The construction boss nodded agreement, then the room emptied and left Jonathan studying her with the cynical expression she'd learned to hate.

He was lounging with one hip on the desk, one long leg hooked over its corner. He was wearing battered jeans and a red cotton shirt open at the throat. Over the shirt he wore a leather jacket hanging open. There was no gypsy in his ancestry but he'd always had the wild look of the gypsy. Years ago he'd laughed when she'd called him one.

It was fourteen years since he'd laughed with her, fourteen years since she'd seen him dressed casually like this. The last time she saw him he'd been intimidating and immaculate in a suit at a charity ball in Toronto. She'd left early and of course they hadn't spoken.

She'd expected the suit again today. He was the architect and he had his own money in this project. He had every right to prowl around in the sort of clothes that ruled out getting his hands dirty.

Architect and entrepreneur, the gypsy boy of her childhood was gone. She had a proposition for the entrepreneur he'd become, not the gypsy of her memories.

Jonathan's gaze made its lazy way from her smoothly imprisoned hair to the polished perfection of her harvest-gold pumps. He gestured towards a wheeled secretary's chair that was sitting in the middle of the office area. 'Have a seat.'

She fought a vision of herself sitting, of Jonathan coming closer, his eyes on her crossed legs. 'No, thanks,' she said stiffly.

All those years ago. . . Lacey Wilkins's party.

Jonathan must have been nineteen, Cynthia sixteen. She'd been warned about him.

When he had come in he had stopped at the door. Frowning. Eyes flicking through the crowd. Then he had walked straight towards Cynthia and she couldn't look away because he was watching her, eyes on her, and he'd ignored the voices calling his name. Ignored everyone but her.

'Moon lady,' he'd said in a low voice as he held out his hand. 'You'd better dance with me. It's time we did something about this.'

She should have said no. Jonathan Halley was trouble but he would mean nothing to her now if she'd said *no* to that first dance. She wouldn't have learned to love him. He wouldn't have ——

Everything would have been different.

Fourteen years, and the mess that had started at Lacey Wilkins's party was still echoing through her life. He was watching her face now and she took in a deep breath and prayed that she could hold his eyes without showing any of her nervousness.

'Moon lady. . .what trouble brings you?'

'Don't call me that.'

She saw amusement flash in his eyes. 'How will you stop me?'

She held his eyes although every instinct fought against it. She'd been well-trained. Don't show a weakness. Never lose a staring match. She might have come begging but she was going to walk out with her head high.

'Nothing's changed,' Jonathan said softly. He pushed one hand roughly through his hair.

She turned away from him and walked to the window. Outside, a cement truck stood with its door open and the driver leaning out. 'Things always change,' she said.

'Perhaps.' She turned to stare at him. He was still lounging on that desk. Still watching her. 'I heard about McAulisson's death,' he said without expression. 'Four years ago. You've stopped wearing his rings. Are you still grieving him?'

She didn't answer.

'Or was your marriage a business arrangement?' His eyes narrowed. 'Dyson Holdings swallowed up McAulisson Press. Perhaps one should call it a merger.'

She realised that her lips were pressed tight and her hands clenched. She forced her fingers to relax, her breathing to steady. Jonathan picked up a tape-measure from the desk and weighed it with one hand. 'Your father wanted control of McAulisson's publishing empire and McAulisson wanted money. You volunteered to be the glue that fixed the deal.' He dropped the tape on the already battered desk. 'Presto. The moon lady gets married. Was that how it was?'

'Is that what you think of me? That I'd sell myself?' She jerked herself away from him, back to the window. Damn Jonathan! It had taken him about two minutes to find a vulnerable spot.

'Why the hell did you marry him?'

Cynthia hugged herself to stop the shiver that wanted to take her body. 'People do marry for love,' she said quietly. The cement truck was moving. Backing up towards a wall of wooden forms. 'Damn you,' she whispered. 'I didn't come here to be battered by you.'

Silence. Long seconds while she focused on the world of construction outside. Where were all the words she'd rehearsed?

'What kind of trouble are you in?' he asked quietly.

She hugged herself tighter. 'What makes you think it's trouble?'

'Why else would you come?'

She could see five men from here, all working at the steady pace that got things done. 'Do they work as hard when you're not here?' she asked.

He didn't answer. She heard papers shuffle and wondered if he was capable of immersing himself in paper with her standing there.

'I imagine it's financial trouble,' he said.

She turned her head and he was watching her. She felt an odd suspension in time. 'Why financial?' she asked.

She and Jonathan. . .

When she was fourteen she'd been thrown from her horse on the hillside below her family home. He'd picked her up and talked to her until he was sure she had her breath. Then he'd gone off and caught the horse and tied it to a bush. They'd sat on the bench by the apple tree afterwards, talking lazily. When she'd asked him what he was doing there he'd laughed and gestured to the tree with its abundant crop of ripening apples.

Then she'd heard her father's car purring along the road, just out of sight.

'Better go,' she'd said urgently. 'My dad will be furious if he catches you.'

He'd laughed and she'd felt fear. Jonathan hadn't changed much since then, she thought. He didn't hesitate to get into battle. From what she'd heard he usually won his fights.

'I don't imagine it's a broken heart,' he said idly.

'No. I wouldn't come to you with a broken heart.'

His eyes flashed with cold humour. 'So it has to be money, doesn't it?'

'You make it sound cold-blooded.'

The lines of his face hardened. He'd always looked roughly handsome but the years had added strength to his eyes and his mouth. As a boy he'd been a force to be reckoned with. Cynthia certainly hadn't been surprised when she'd started seeing Jonathan's name on the boards of directors of some of the companies she dealt with.

His eyes took another sweep of her immaculate suit. 'If you've come here because you missed me and thought you'd drop in —' his smile was ironic — 'the body language is all wrong, moon lady. You're wearing your breeding like a suit of armour. All your rich-girl training is showing. That snobbish bun you've knotted your hair into. The family pearls around your throat.'

Her fingers went to the pearls. 'I did come to talk business. Why——' She gestured around the construction office. 'Why don't I take you out to dinner? We could——'

'I wouldn't want to take your money under false pretences. Why don't you state your business first?'

'Right,' she agreed, vowing to be every bit as inscrutable as the man watching her. She stiffened her shoulders.

Someone shouted his name from outside. The door slammed open and the man with the orange hard-hat called in, 'Jonathan! We're ready to pour!'

'On my way,' said Jonathan. His eyes met Cynthia's. 'You'll wait?'

She nodded.

His lips twitched. 'Twenty minutes,' he said. 'I'll be back.'

It was crazy to feel as if he'd just asked her not to go. As if it were personal. She had to keep the past firmly separated from here and now. She hadn't realised he would affect her like this. When he was gone she crossed her arms over her midriff and paced the construction office. She prowled behind the counter and stood staring at a black leather briefcase standing in one corner.

It wasn't worth the risk. The contents wouldn't tell her any of Jonathan's secrets, and if he caught her——

What if he said no?

Fourteen years ago when she'd faced him across the battered width of his own front porch he hadn't shown an ounce of caring for her. She'd pounded on his door and eventually he'd come out with his hair tousled and his chest naked and he'd told her to get out of his life.

She'd been insane to come today.

Jonathan Halley wouldn't do a damned thing to help her.

But surely he felt some responsibility towards Allan? Or had the Jonathan she'd once loved disappeared completely? The Jonathan who cared, who took action when he saw things that weren't fair. Perhaps that Jonathan had never really existed but she'd believed in him once.

Until he told her to get out of his life.

The only sensible thing was to believe that Jonathan Halley was a bastard. But if that was true there was no point to her coming here today.

Footsteps on the stairs outside. She dropped her arms as she saw the door opening. She felt the impact as he came through the door and suddenly the room was too crowded.

'Can we go for a walk?' she asked. 'Outside somewhere?'

His eyes flickered over her. He stopped at the counter filled with its confusion of blueprints and rested one hand on a blueprint roll.

'Spit it out, moon lady. What do you want of me?'

She bit her lip. She saw his gaze fix on her mouth and her spine snapped to attention. 'Right,' she said. She hoped her voice was as brisk as his. 'I came to offer you an interest in the Synerson Syndicate.'

His black brows lowered in a way that made a shiver run down her spine. 'You invested in that mess?'

'I —— Not directly.'

'Too speculative?' His lips twisted ironically. 'You never did like taking risks, did you?'

Of all the men in the world, Jonathan was the only one who had ever had the power to make her lose her temper. She met his eyes coolly now and she was almost positive that he couldn't see her anger.

'I didn't come to discuss my judgement as an investor.'

He grinned. 'Didn't your father teach you to talk nicely when you ask for money?'

Anger crawled along her veins. 'It's Allan's investment,' she snapped.

'Ah,' he said softly. A muscle flexed in his jaw. 'So that is brother Allan's mess. Why isn't he the one asking me for help?'

She felt a wild urge to pace and fought it. She slipped her hands into the big pockets of her suit jacket. Jonathan's eyes followed the motion as if he knew she'd clenched her fists under cover of the fabric.

'Allan doesn't like asking for help,' she said, 'But I——'

'He seems to have asked you.' Jonathan was watching her through narrowed eyes.

'He needs your help,' she said doggedly.

'I'm not lifting a finger for your brother.'

Cynthia walked stiffly to the water-cooler in the corner. She picked up a paper cup and filled it. She stood with her back to him so that he wouldn't see her hand shaking as she drank slowly. He was watching her. Waiting for her reaction.

'You're a bastard,' she said quietly. 'If it weren't for my father you wouldn't have anything today. This hotel you've invested in, that office tower in Vancouver, the conference centre back east. . .this island in the Mediterranean——if you'd gotten what you deserved——'

'What do you imagine I deserved?'

She turned to face him. He was watching her with brows lowered and eyes narrowed. She remembered him staring at her that way when she was sixteen. Staring at her while he destroyed her with words.

'I'd hoped you'd help.' She put the paper cup down. She'd been crazy to come. She swallowed, and muttered, 'If my father had filed against you for damages you'd still be paying.'

'Don't be naïve, moon lady. If he'd had grounds he would have sued.'

She felt as if she was back on his porch all those years ago. Confused and hurt. 'Don't you feel any responsibility to Allan?' she whispered.

'None at all.' When he smiled she shivered because there was something dangerous about that smile. 'When you get back to Toronto I suggest that you call your brother and give him a message from me.'

Her heart was pounding as if he'd made a threat.

'Tell him Jonathan said not to send you asking for money again.'

'He didn't send me. I came on my own.' She dropped the paper cup into a bin. 'I've had enough of this,' she said stiffly. 'I'm leaving.'

A handsome man who smiled easily for other people. He wasn't smiling for her now. He asked, 'Does Allan's mess matter that much to you?'

'Do you think I'd ask you if it didn't? The last time I saw you, you made some snide remark about my coming to you when I needed you.' She gulped and glared at him. 'I vowed the last damned thing I'd ever do was come begging to you. I should have kept that vow.'

'You're here,' he pointed out. 'So sit down. Tell me the details.'

'You said you wouldn't lift a finger for Allan.'

He was smiling, not frowning. 'I might do it for *you*,' he said. 'Sit down, Cynthia.'

She sat slowly. 'You've never done anything for

anyone in my family,' she said. She lifted her eyes and
he was watching her. She flushed because he'd watched
her exactly that way down on the Connars' farm during
the haying.

He leaned back against the desk. 'How deep is Allan
in the Synerson deal?'

She named a sum and he whistled softly.

'The fool.'

She curled her hands around the arms of the chair.
'He said you were in it. He said it was a sure thing
because you had bought in.'

'But you didn't invest?'

She shook her head. 'It's not my sort of thing. I
imagine you've got some sort of inside knowledge
about where that highway's going to go. For all I know
you bribed someone to get that information——'

'Your brother is a fool,' he said grimly. 'I'm not in
that syndicate. I looked at it but anyone would be
insane to gamble on the environmental study coming
out positive. And, despite your feelings about my
ethics, I have no idea which route that highway's
going.' His face was shuttered. 'I don't bribe public
officials but it wouldn't surprise me if the syndicate
hasn't spread money around. But an unfavourable
election could turn a good prospect into so much
useless real estate. I suppose he gave someone a note
to cover the commitment?'

'Yes. Garth Synerson.'

Jonathan's jaw went hard. 'Let him face the music,'
he suggested softly. 'It's time someone let Allan pay
for his own mistakes.'

She bit her lip, then released it, as a widening of
Jonathan's eyes made her aware of how revealing a
gesture that was. 'I can't do that,' she said tonelessly.
'He's my brother.' She wished she'd kept her paper
cup. Something to turn in her hands.

Jonathan was frowning, looking towards the window as if he wished he could be back out there with the contractors. She realised that it wasn't going to work. He'd refused to leave the work site with her. Refused her offer of a meal. He wasn't willing to spend more than a few minutes on her and he certainly wouldn't hand over any money.

He pushed himself up and went to the desk. He opened a drawer and pulled out a bottle and two glasses. 'Whisky, moon lady?'

She shook her head.

His mouth twitched in what might be the beginning of a smile. 'One drink? You're hardly risking those valuable inhibitions.'

She shook her head, fighting memories.

'Inhibitions,' he had murmured softly as his fingers had traced from the edge of her mouth to the sensitive place just behind her ear. Her pulse had trembled with the journey of his touch over her flesh. His eyes had held hers. 'We could do something about those inhibitions. You and I, together.'

Memories. . .

She had to stop this! She cleared her throat and said tightly, 'I'm not about to let loose with the whisky when I'm negotiating with you. I'm not foolish.'

He lifted the glass to his lips.

'This is a waste of time,' she said restlessly. 'I'll go. I'll —— '

'Why doesn't Allan approach me himself?'

'I imagine he hates you. After what you did to him —— '

Jonathan twisted the glass in his hand. 'What did I do to him?'

'For heaven's sake, Jonathan! You know! You —— '

'Talk nicely when you want money,' he suggested softly.

'Damn you!'

His throat flexed as he swallowed the rest of the whisky. She glared at him and was suddenly aware of her own breathing. Too rapid. And the tension in her face. Jonathan was watching, as if he'd thrown a grenade into the conversation and was waiting for her to react.

'Damn you,' she whispered. 'You did that deliberately. You always want to throw me off balance.' She pushed the anger back. Anger wouldn't get her anywhere with him. 'Score one for you,' she said quietly.

'That's what I always liked about you,' he said softly. 'You don't stay down. How badly do you want Allan's mess straightened out?'

'Badly enough to come to you.' She quieted her breathing and kept her body very still. She smelled danger. 'Are we negotiating?'

'Perhaps.'

Suddenly the counter between them felt like a boardroom table, strong conflicting interests and the moment of quiet before the balance of power changed.

'I came asking for help.' She deliberately locked the tension out of her voice. 'I don't have anything to bargain with.'

He put the glass down. 'How badly do you want to bail Allan out?'

She studied the deep lines on both sides of Jonathan's mouth. She touched her ear and caught her pearl stud between thumb and forefinger. 'What is it you want?' she asked warily. 'A piece of Dyson Holdings?'

'Allan doesn't have any of Dyson to sell me. He sold the last shares on the open market two years ago. Two years before that he sold a block to you.'

She frowned. 'Why would you know that?'

'I keep track,' he said. 'What's different about this

bad investment? It's not Allan's first disaster. What makes you desperate enough to come to me?'

'I'm not desperate.' She dropped her hand from the earring. It wasn't a good bargaining position, letting the other party know you were in danger of bankruptcy. Letting Jonathan know.

He smiled, an ironic twist of his lips. 'Five years ago you said you would roast in hell before you'd ask me for anything. What's changed?'

She shivered. 'I'm offering you an interest in Synerson. A business deal. Not——'

He studied her until she felt the urge to move restlessly growing wild inside her. 'Shares in Synerson aren't worth the paper they're written on.'

'All right, then. I——' She stood up abruptly and admitted, 'I guaranteed Allan's note.' She didn't need the widening of his eyes to know he thought her a fool.

'Personally?' he asked.

'Yes.' She swallowed. 'And Dyson Holdings.'

He let out a long whistle. 'You really don't learn, do you, moon lady?'

CHAPTER TWO

JONATHAN HALLEY had always been a gambling man — not irrational wagers, but calculated acts of risk. He knew that there was sacrifice and benefit in every deal. He always tried to weigh the two and come out ahead.

In the last few years he'd made deals that had made him millions. Once, when he was a kid of nineteen, he'd made a deal that had lost him Cynthia Dyson-Paige. He'd made the bargain and he'd kept his promise, but he didn't like it. And now Cynthia had come to him and the irony was that she wanted to bail her brother out of trouble.

'They've called the note?' he asked.

'Yes.' She sat down again slowly. He understood what that meant. She had no other options. 'Last Friday,' she said. 'He can't cover it.'

'How much?'

She was playing with that earring again. No expression in her face but her body gave her away. Tension. Desperation. He fought the urge to reach for her. To touch her. She named a figure.

'Your shares in Dyson Holdings wouldn't cover that.'

Her eyes flared. 'Do you have my net worth on file?'

There wasn't much he didn't know about her. Except why she'd married Eric McAulisson. Business or love, they'd been married six years before McAulisson had died of an early heart attack. Husband and wife. Jonathan knew it was insane to speculate on the details, yet the vision of Cynthia entangled in passion with McAulisson had tormented him through too many dreams.

He didn't want to believe in it.

'I'll cover the note,' he said, 'but there is a condition.'

She might have been a statue. Only her eyes were alive. He spread his hands, fighting the urge to lean across and pull her hair free of the ridiculous knot she'd twisted it into. He remembered her hair falling to her waist, remembered taking every pin out of it and kissing her until she was breathing wild and soft with chestnut waves a curtain all around them and his hands sliding through the silk.

He took slow, rigid breaths to tame his heartbeat.

Damn! Not now!

'What condition?' Her eyes met his directly.

He'd always liked her directness, the way she had steel under the soft woman's skin.

'I want you to marry me, moon lady.'

He saw her hand clench. Her fingers were white but colour crawled into her face from her throat.

'You're crazy,' she whispered.

Outside, someone shouted. Jonathan heard the sound of the cement truck pumping. Cynthia was breathing too rapidly. Her hands clenched and then she jerked her fingers open. He lowered his eyelids to mask whatever might show in his eyes. She had to know he wanted her but he masked his feelings, anyway. It was habit with her. Because she knew how to strike at him in ways no one else ever had. Because he had secrets that even now he couldn't share with her.

'No!' she said sharply, then, 'Why? It doesn't make sense.' A tendril of long, glossy hair escaped and she lifted one hand to tuck it neatly away behind her ear.

Maybe she didn't have pins in her hair. If he took out that clasp at the back, would the whole luxurious mass come tumbling into his hands? Taking Cynthia's

hair down had once had a disastrous effect on the wall
of her inhibitions. Kissing those dark, full lips, teasing
the stiffness out of her until the woman inside came
loose. Cynthia. . .confronting her under the old apple
tree near her house. . .touching her shoulder and hearing the gasp she couldn't contain. . .then that one
spinning moment of anger when he'd understood
everything.

Damn!

The past was gone. Beyond changing.

But today she'd come to *him* for help.

He shoved a rough hand through his hair. 'Those are
the only terms I'm offering,' he said slowly.

'Are you saying——' she had to clear her throat and
he saw the colour climb higher in her cheeks '——you—
you'll cover Allan's note if I—if I. . .?'

'If you marry me. Yes.'

She stood up again and began to pace. 'Why on
earth would you want to marry me? I don't even——'
Her throat spasmed and for a second her eyes couldn't
hold his. 'We've hardly spoken to each other in years!
You don't—this has to be a joke.'

He stood and placed his hand flat on the counter.
'It's not a joke. Call it a gamble if you like.' He didn't
see that he had a lot to lose. Just money. And if he
won——

'What do you get out of it?' Her voice turned brittle.
'What do you want? The Paige connections?'

He leaned forward. 'I don't give a damn that your
mother was Cassandra Paige. And you can be sure it's
not your money I want.' He smiled grimly. 'If you
don't say yes you'll be bankrupt—and if you do I'll
have a bloody nightmare straightening out Synerson.'

'Then *why*?'

'I want you.'

She choked off the gasp. 'I thought for Allan. . .

Don't you think you owe him?' Her hands were tangled together in front of her. Her eyes were wide and shocked as if she had lost the ability to dissemble. Jonathan figured that that would last for about two minutes before she got her walls firmly back in place.

He tightened his grip on the blueprints. 'I don't owe Allan a damned thing. If I bail him out for you I'll tie him in a financial knot while I do it. Your bloody brother has ruined enough lives. He won't do this to you again.'

'He's crippled,' whispered Cynthia.

He smiled grimly. 'You're saying that's my fault?'

'No,' she breathed. 'No. I—of course it was an accident.'

He pushed aside the roll of blueprints. The accident had been in the timing. Allan too damned drunk to stand up and Cynthia's father in a towering rage. He couldn't hear Cynthia's voice but her mouth made the words plainly.

'No. I won't. I won't marry you.'

'Where are you staying?' he asked. He knew when to stop pushing.

'Estuary Motel.'

He arranged the rolls of blueprints at one end of the counter, keeping his hands busy because otherwise he might cross the space between them and touch her, to try to drown out the worry in her green eyes. He'd dreamed her eyes in every way they could look. Wide with discovery. Flecked with gold and angry as spit. Darkened with apprehension. Narrowed by suspicion and betrayal.

He'd lose if he reached for her now.

If he waited. . .

She would go back to her motel. She would think about letting the corporation her father founded go down the tubes. About letting her brother lose everything. About filing bankruptcy herself.

'I've got work to do,' he said. 'We'll talk later.'

'No,' she said. She shook her head decisively. 'If that's—no.'

'I'll pick you up for dinner. Eight o'clock.'

The anger flashed into her eyes. She drew in a hissing breath. 'I'm not selling myself to you, Jonathan! I'm on the next ferry off this island.'

He couldn't stop himself reaching for her as she stepped towards the door. She froze under his touch, her nostrils flared and her breathing tight and quick. He could feel her arm trembling through the fabric of her jacket. What would happen if he pulled her into his arms?

'I'll pick you up at eight,' he said, and felt her tension increase. 'You don't have any choices, moon lady.'

No choices. Damn Jonathan!

She didn't let the trembling start until she was safely inside the motel room. Then, with her hands shaking and her heart pounding, she dialled Toronto and listened to the ringing signal on Allan's phone.

Jonathan wanted her. She felt a shiver deep inside. Of course, she'd known when she was sixteen that he wanted her. He hadn't hidden it then. But *he* was the one who had sent her away!

Another life. Another world.

'*Those are the only terms I'm offering.*'

Marriage in exchange for his money. Insane! Whatever she had to do to get out of this mess, she wasn't marrying Jonathan Halley!

Allan answered his telephone on the eleventh ring.

'Do you have any idea what time it is?' he demanded.

'Do *you* have any news?' She felt a wave of dizziness.

'Like winning the lottery or hearing that someone burned your promissory note?'

He sighed, and she knew the news wasn't good. 'Garth phoned,' he said wearily.

Cynthia closed her eyes and she could picture her brother. His face would be discouraged and his hand rubbing his left leg absently as he spoke. He might be watching his cane out of one eye as if he was aware of the effort it would take to get to his feet.

'I don't suppose Garth offered you an extension on the note?'

'No. He said our three days of grace are up.'

No escape. No way out.

'Expect to hear from his lawyer on Monday,' said Allan.

She could see the ocean through the window. Slow waves coming in. A sailboat out in the deep water, white sails against the blue sky. 'You haven't come up with any way to get the money?' she asked. 'Have you thought of anything?'

'It's hardly my fault,' he said plaintively. 'If I'd had more time——'

It was useless expecting Allan to find his own way back to solvency. She sighed and said, 'Jonathan figures those shares you've got are worth about as much as a lottery ticket.'

'Jonathan Halley?' Attention snapped into his voice. 'You've been talking to Jonathan? Why? When?'

She closed the fingers of one hand, making a fist. 'An hour ago.'

'Stay away from him, Cyn.' He muttered a curse. 'Keep out of his way.'

She stared at the white flesh of her own fist. She squeezed her fingers tighter together and the whiteness spread. 'Why should I stay away from Jonathan? You said he was an investor in Synerson. I thought he might be willing to buy you out.'

'Garth says Jonathan backed out.' She heard the sound of a lighter and realised that Allan had just lit a cigarette. 'If he'd stayed in, the project wouldn't be going down now.'

'Going down.' She closed her eyes and wondered what she would do after she had sold everything to meet Allan's note. According to Jonathan, Allan would own a big share of nothing and meanwhile the creditors would still be pounding on Dyson's doors.

According to Jonathan he'd never been *in* on the Synerson deal and Allan's problems were all Allan's fault.

'You're smoking again,' she accused although it was ludicrous to bother about Allan's smoking when they were on the verge of bankruptcy.

'You didn't ask him for the money?' demanded Allan. 'Tell me you didn't.'

'Don't you think he owes you?'

'Oh, lord, Cyn!' Allan sounded frightened and that made no sense at all.

'He said to give you a message.' She let her fist loose. 'He said you weren't to send me asking for money again.'

'It wasn't my idea! Tell him I didn't know you were ——'

'Allan? Why would you be scared of him?' She bit her lip. 'Did he ever threaten you, back when —— ?'

'Cyn! Stay out of it! Stay away from Jonathan.'

She'd heard that before.

Stay away from that Halley kid. If you don't ——

'Find some other way to get the money,' Allan pleaded. 'Sell shares. Do whatever you have to, but don't ask Jonathan Halley.'

She sighed. 'In that case you'd better come up with

something else because I don't have any other bright ideas to bail us out of this.'

Jonathan had said that she didn't learn and maybe that was true. Because she'd signed that guarantee for Allan and he wasn't going to do anything to help them out of this mess now. He'd handed the problem to her. Maybe he believed she owed it to him to bail him out. Any maybe she did owe Allan, because her father's will had been grossly unfair.

'Because I'm adopted,' Allan had muttered bitterly when the will was read. 'And you're the real thing.'

At one time their father had treated them equally, but in the last years before his death he'd become bitter about her older brother. As if he hated him. Maybe it was part of the bitterness and anger that had seemed to consume him after their mother died, but it was terribly unfair on Allan. Cynthia had done what she could to make up for the injustice, but Allan wasn't good with money and it had begun to seem that there was no end to it.

Until now, and if Garth went the full extent of the law on Cynthia's personal guarantee both she and Dyson Holdings would be filing bankruptcy. There weren't any options. The bank wasn't going to advance her the amount she needed without more security. She was already mortgaged heavily on the development of a residential suburb outside Toronto.

Right now she didn't have one unencumbered marketable commodity to trade on except for her shares, and they weren't enough to pay off the promissory note. If she sold them she would have nothing. Dyson Holdings would be gone, probably broken up. She would be looking for a job. There weren't that many jobs begging for people like her. She'd been 'finished' in Switzerland and trained in management. Upper-management jobs were disappearing like stones in the

ocean these days. And — well, she'd liked being her
own boss. And — damn it! — she'd done a reasonable
job of running Dyson Holdings.

'You don't have any choices' Jonathan had said. As
if he knew the details of her affairs.

No marketable assets. Except one. Herself.

Jonathan Halley wanted her badly enough to bail
Allan out in return for marriage. It didn't make sense.
She'd read enough articles about him, the young mil-
lionaire who avoided commitments with women. She'd
heard gossip, women with young, wealthy daughters
angling after Jonathan. But not her. Never her. She'd
been sold at the altar of business once before. She was
damned if she'd let it happen again.

She walked to the window and stared out at the
beach. Sunshine. Late afternoon. She'd told Jonathan
she was checking out and she would, but first she would
walk on that beach.

She slipped her heels and tights off. Then she
dropped the earrings on the bed and added the necklace. Mother's pearls. She'd worn them to Lacey's
party and Jonathan had recognised them today. It
bothered her that he should remember them. She
shivered and pulled the clasp out of her hair. Then she
shed the jacket to her suit. She was left in the harvest-
gold skirt, a short-sleeved white silk blouse and bare
feet. Shorts and a T-shirt would make more sense for
the beach but she'd brought clothes for facing
Jonathan, not beachwear.

She walked slowly through the sand, feeling the way
it held her back, the way she sank in and the warmth
that gave way to coolness when her toes wiggled deeper
down. A breath of wind caught her long hair and sent
it flying around her head. She tamed it with her hands.

The water caressed the sand in long, slow swells.
There were whitecaps out in the strait, but here on the

beach was only the slow echo of what the wind had done to the ocean. She walked into the water and let the cool sea rise up to her calves. The sand sucked away under her feet as she walked, the world eroding away, drawing her bare feet down. She hadn't felt that sensation in years, not since childhood summers here on Vancouver Island.

She turned and looked back along the beach. She could see a woman walking hand in hand with a child of about six. Cynthia shivered. Mother and daughter. The thought reminded her of too many failed dreams.

When she was eighteen, she'd fallen ill and been hospitalised in a clinic in Europe. Before discharging her from the clinic, the doctors had run a series of tests. The results had shown that she was infertile. She'd cried when she heard because once she had dreamed of having Jonathan Halley's children. Jonathan had been gone from her life since she was sixteen, but some small part of the dream had remained and brought tears.

With time, her feelings for Jonathan had turned to a numb knot deep inside her. She would never love like that again, would never lose herself so completely as she had in Jonathan's arms. But she'd vowed that one day she would care for another man. Not the wild insanity of Jonathan, but the sane warmth of a mature woman's affections.

She had been twenty when she met Eric. Twenty when she'd married him. She hadn't been home in four years then, four years of finishing school and visits to friends in Europe, broken by the months of her illness when she was eighteen. Four years of painful dreams of Jonathan. Lonely years, but she had believed that she'd finally put the memories of Jonathan behind her.

Then, one day, Eric McAulisson had come to the Mediterranean villa where she was staying with a schoolfriend. The maid had called her and she'd gone to the door. When the handsome blonde man had smiled at her she had smiled back.

He introduced himself with a charming smile. 'Your father said I should look you up on my way through Europe.'

He worked in news, he'd said. Usually Cynthia was bored by the people her father sent to check up on her, but Eric was different. He was charming, intelligent and had seemed interested in Cynthia for herself rather than her father's money.

He had courted her with determination and charm. She'd told herself that Jonathan was the insanity of her youth, that Eric was what she wanted for a lifetime. But when he had proposed she knew she had to tell him there would never be children.

'Children aren't important to me,' he'd said. He'd sounded so uninterested that she'd felt rebuffed. Maybe he didn't even *like* children.

She hadn't told him about Jonathan. There had been no reason. Her first love was dead and deeply buried. She felt affection for Eric. Deeper love would grow with time.

The wedding had come too quickly.

Her father had flown to Europe, a one-day trip so that he could walk her up the aisle. He'd sent an employee ahead to arrange the event. Cynthia was married from her father's Paris house. She had felt unreal in the church, perhaps because she hadn't seen her father or this house in four years and her feelings about him were so mixed. As she'd walked up the aisle on his arm, she had had a horrifying feeling that she was making a terrible mistake.

She didn't remember saying the vows. Her memories of her wedding-day focused on afterwards. The reception. Eric's ring on her finger and herself listening to one of the guests talking. She'd caught sight of Eric and her father going into the library and abruptly her unease had focused into a sudden, sick certainty.

Eric and her father closeted in the study after the wedding.

She had followed.

When she'd opened the study door they were standing close together by the window. Eric was just replacing his wallet in the inside breast pocket of his dinner-jacket. When he saw her he had jerked back two paces.

Her father had turned his head and stared at her with eyebrows raised, pointing out in silence that she was interrupting.

'I'd like to see what you just put in your wallet,' she said to Eric.

Her husband flushed.

Her father said, 'Cynthia, you're being hysterical. Get back to your guests.'

From the time her mother died, her father had trained her to be polite to important guests. Now she only shook her head and asked quietly, 'How much did he pay you to marry me, Eric?'

Eric's flush deepened and she knew she was right. . .

'You sold me,' she accused her father. When his head jerked up she was caught in an instant of terror, as if she were a child disobeying him again. Then the rage in his eyes shut down and he was watching her as if she were an insect that had crawled into his study.

'You sold me to Eric. His influence in the media for your money! It's true, isn't it?' She didn't know what she expected. Denial perhaps, but he said nothing.

She sank down into the big chair on the far side of the desk from the two men, her father and the man she'd married. Asking *why* was pointless. Business had always come first with her father and influence with the media was an asset for a man who was always upsetting environmentalists and government bureaucrats.

'You're married,' he said in a voice that held a threat.

'You used my life as if it were a commodity. How could you ——?' Something flickered in his eyes and, although Jonathan was the past and she'd stopped hurting from those wounds, she heard herself ask, 'You made Jonathan stop seeing me, didn't you?'

'Jonathan Halley was no good.' His eyes went flat and hard. 'He was never any good. Keep away from him. You'll stay married to Eric.'

She held his eyes and felt a shiver of fear.

'Cynthia ——' Eric's voice was hesitant. 'I'm very fond of you. I wouldn't have asked you to marry me if I weren't.'

'Yes,' she agreed, because she'd walked into this with her eyes open. She'd agreed to marry Eric knowing that his affection for her was mild. It was what she'd thought she wanted. A sane, safe relationship. She was the one who had refused to listen to her own doubts. She'd made her vows and she would keep them.

Jonathan was right. She'd been sold into marriage with Eric but she'd been too much of a fool to realise what was happening until the vows were said. She'd been miles away from her father when she met Eric and it hadn't occurred to her that her romance was orchestrated by her father's business plans.

She'd played the part that had been written for her. They had honeymooned in Venice, where Eric had agreed to her request for separate rooms. When they returned to Toronto where Eric had his home, Cynthia had moved into his house and taken on the obligations of his very political social life. She had insisted on separate bedrooms, and Eric had agreed without argument.

Shortly after her return to Toronto, she had gone to her father's office and asked him to put her to work in Dyson Holdings. 'If you're using me as an asset in this business,' she'd said, 'then I should be involved in it.'

Her father, rather surprisingly, had agreed and Cynthia had learned that she had abilities in business that she'd never dreamed of. Her days had become filled with the business of Dyson Holdings. Evenings, she'd usually had some social event to attend with Eric, who had been preparing to run for mayor in the next election.

In the six years of her artificial marriage to Eric, they had never fought and seldom disagreed. They had lived together as polite, courteous friends and in the end, when Eric died a year after her father, she had cried for him. He'd been a good man and her friend. She'd helped him in his failed bid for the mayoralty, and she'd been sorry when he'd lost. Sorry when he died, and sad because her life hardly seemed to change with her husband's death. She'd lost a friend. She'd never had a husband.

She felt as if she had been alone all her life, even during the years of her shell of a marriage. Her own woman, but now, after all these years, she'd come begging to Jonathan Halley.

She kicked at the sand and drew in a big gulp of sea air. She had no choice, Jonathan had said, but there had to be a choice. She'd have to sell Dyson. She didn't want to. She'd got rid of her father's doubtful investments now, and she wanted to see the new subdivision in The Heights to completion. She'd fought her father for that kind of development, with facilities for community recreation and day-care. A subdivision for middle-class people to live a quality life in, with things for the young and a window on the world for the stay-at-home mothers.

She kicked the sand again and behind her a voice said softly, 'It wouldn't be that bad.'

Her heart jammed up in her throat.

She spun around to face him. He was standing five feet away, his hands in the pocket of his jeans and his jacket bunched up over his wrists. There was a look in his eyes as if he might smile, if she curved her lips first.

'You mean because I've done it before?' The wind blew her hair across her eyes. Her voice was as harsh as she could make it. 'Is that what you're implying?'

'Is that how it was with McAulisson? Were you forced to marry him?'

'Don't be ridiculous!' She hugged herself tightly. 'I wanted to marry Eric! But you——'

'You're desperate, moon lady. And you can trust me.'

She swallowed. 'Saying I can trust you is. . .' An astounding statement, she'd meant to say. A lie. 'Trust you how?' she asked faintly.

'To keep whatever bargain we make.'

'Bargain?' She shook her head and the hair went wild in the wind. 'You mean we'd negotiate a contract? A *written* contract?'

'If you want.'

A pre-nuptial agreement. 'You'd tie me in knots,' she said wildly. 'I'd be mad.'

'Name the terms you want. We'll discuss it.'

'But you *already* named the terms!'

One side of his mouth curved in a half-smile. 'You're a different person with your hair down, moon lady.'

She made an explosive sound. She wanted to laugh because it was ridiculous. The whole thing was ridiculous. 'You want me,' she said. She could hear the edges of hysteria in her own voice. 'You said—you meant ——' He watched her stumble through the words and she thought he was amused. 'Sexually,' she said. 'You meant sexually.'

'Hmm.' His eyes were laughing. 'Among other things, yes.'

She flushed and turned away. She couldn't see the far shore, couldn't see the mainland because of a haze over the water. She muttered, 'My terms would be — my own bed and you stay out of it. Out of my bed. No — no sex.'

'You want a blanket guarantee? No sex in any circumstances?'

'Damn you!' she snapped angrily. She glared at him but the laughter was still there in his eyes.

'Come on, moon lady! How about a compromise?'

'What compromise?' She could feel the heat in her face and she felt like a fool. Damn Jonathan!

He shrugged and suggested, 'The marriage won't be consummated unless you request it.'

'Unless I — I wouldn't. Never!'

'Then you're in no danger, are you?'

'You'd be wasting your money.'

'That's my problem, isn't it?' He met her eyes with a challenge in his.

This was insane! She couldn't be negotiating marriage with Jonathan! 'I have a business,' she said. 'I'm not giving that up.' That was insane, too, because when she got home she was going to have to put her shares on the market.

'Of course,' he agreed.

She frowned. He was being far too agreeable. 'You're saying that we could have a ceremony and I can just walk away? That would be the end of it?'

'No.' There was steel in his eyes. 'When you have to be in Toronto you live under my roof. You live under my roof at all times. My condo in Toronto, my apartment in Vancouver.'

She swallowed. 'I don't——'

'That's not negotiable.' Jonathan was taking the gloves off now, his eyes hard and his mouth grim. He'd taken his hands out of his pockets and she was intensely aware that he could touch her if he took only one step.

'Anything else that's not negotiable?' she asked. She wasn't crazy enough to do it. There had to be another answer. She'd go into the village and find a lottery-ticket vendor. She'd win a million and that would be the end of the problem.

'Yes,' he said. 'There's more. There'll be no snide magazine articles about the sham of our marriage. When your business interests and mine allow, we'll be together. We'll both play the part and we'll play it well. Under the same roof.'

'I don't——'

'And if there's a child,' he said grimly, 'we'll live in the country. You can choose which province, which country even. But rural. We're not bringing up a child in the city. I won't expect you to give up your business interests entirely, but if we have a child we'll bring it up together, and don't get that look in your eyes, because there'll be no divorce if you have my child.'

Oh, God. . .

'There won't be a child,' she said stiffly.

He smiled wryly. 'There could come a day when you invite me into your bed. I'm gambling that you will.'

'There won't be a child. I won't—and even——' She shook her head. 'Once Allan is out of the woods I'll divorce you.'

He grinned and reached out one hand to brush her wind-blown hair away from her face. 'In your dreams, moon lady. When I buy that note of Allan's, he'll owe me. Do you really imagine he'll ever pay me off?'

'But aren't you ——?' She jerked away from his touch on her hair. 'I thought you'd buy his shares in Synerson.'

He shook his head sharply. 'Personally I'd prefer to bring down that project. The whole Synerson lot are as crooked as they come. Including your brother.' His smile disappeared and he said softly, 'But you're not. You never were and when you sign our agreement I promise you I'll honour it just as I know you will.'

It wasn't a game. For a minute it had seemed a game to play, challenging her wits against Jonathan's. 'You think I'll agree?' she asked in a husky voice.

'You're here,' he pointed out. He turned, and his body blocked the wind so that they were staring at each other across an artificial calm.

'We're talking about it. That's all.' She shivered. 'I warn you, I drive a hard bargain.'

'So do I,' he said with a grin. 'But I do intend to make certain we don't regret it.'

CHAPTER THREE

THEY signed the contract in Warren Liturson's office twenty storeys above the ground in Vancouver's financial district. The office was located in Jonathan's building. Liturson was Jonathan's lawyer and Cynthia would have been willing to hire him for anything that needed discretion. From the expression on his face they could have been signing a land deal instead of an agreement that exchanged a large sum of Jonathan's money for Cynthia's participation in an act of marriage.

'I prepared it myself,' Liturson murmured as he passed out a copy of the contract to Jonathan and one to Cynthia.

Cynthia hid a nervous smile. No secretary to leak the terms of the marriage to the public. She bit her lip and read. Everything they had discussed was here but she'd thought of a wealth of things that might be there — and weren't. She looked up and met Jonathan's eyes. She wasn't sure what their gazes said to each other in that long, sober exchange.

If she was going to back out this was the moment to do it. Once she signed that paper there was no way out. Maybe she could run from the wedding-ceremony on Friday, but this was the real decision point. If she signed this contract Jonathan would trust her to fulfil her end of the bargain.

'You're getting a bad deal,' she said soberly. From the corner of her eye she saw the lawyer move abruptly as if he agreed. 'You're giving up a pile of money and you're not getting much in return.'

'We'll see,' he said. He leaned across to the desk and

picked up a black pen from the holder on the desk. He
turned to the last page of his copy and deliberately
scrawled his signature. Then he held out the pen to
her.

A thousand questions flooded through her mind.
Unanswered questions. The man waiting for her to
take the pen was one with the boy who had locked eyes
with her at Lacey's party. She raised her eyes to his
and her heart stopped. She knew where this would end
just as as she had known the night he took her out of
Lacey's party. There had always been something in
Jonathan that took her will away from her. . .made her
ready to discard caution and let the storm determine
her fate.

She jerked her gaze away from his eyes. Warren
Liturson was watching. Endless time, as if Jonathan
had been holding that pen out to her forever and she
were balanced on the edge of a precipice. And it was a
real danger because Jonathan's eyes still had the power
to do that to her. She looked down at the paper in her
hand and the words steadied her breathing.

It was a business deal. Jonathan was the one making
a mistake, not Cynthia. He was gambling that one day
she would choose to make their marriage real. She
would have to *ask* him to make love to her for there to
be any danger.

And he'd just signed. So, if she trusted Jonathan's
word, she was perfectly safe. She took the pen from his
hand. He pushed the copy he'd just signed towards her
and she quickly signed her name under his. Inside she
was shaking but her hand was steady.

'You'll contact Garth Synerson?' she said.

Jonathan's black eyes flickered to the lawyer.

'It's arranged,' the lawyer's neutral voice announced.
'I spoke to Synerson's lawyer an hour ago.'

She stared at the pen in her hand. She'd just signed

the second copy of the contract. She felt a wave of relief. The prospect of Garth's lawyer appearing at her office in Toronto today had haunted her.

'What if I'd changed my mind?' she asked Jonathan. Something flickered in his eyes and she felt the air freeze in her lungs. 'You'd have picked up the note anyway?' She couldn't read the answer from his eyes but she knew him well enough to know that he wouldn't have approached Garth about buying Allan's note until he'd made an unchangeable decision. 'For Allan?' she whispered but he shook his head.

'Sign the last copy so we can get out of here.' He had scrawled his signature on the copy that had been in the lawyer's hands and was waiting for the one she'd just signed.

He would have helped her anyway but he wasn't doing it for Allan no matter what she thought he should feel towards her brother. He was doing it for her. She stared down at the pen still in her hand and reached for the last copy. If she hadn't signed she would still owe Jonathan. There was no way she'd ever be able to pay him back. If she liquidated all her assets it couldn't cover Allan's note and she'd be left still owing with no way to repay the debt.

Better this way. A shell of a marriage, but it was what he'd asked for. It wasn't as if she had any intention of marrying again. Of falling in love. She certainly wasn't going to fall in love with this man again. She glanced at Jonathan and thought wryly that there could be worse things than playing the part of his wife. He was dressed in a suit today, but somehow he wore formality with the same casual masculine grace that she associated with Jonathan in jeans and leather jackets. She liked watching him, maybe even liked the way he made her feel alive and endangered both at once.

'Lunch,' he said as they left the lawyer's office.

'I'll buy.' When laughter flickered over his face she realised how militant she sounded.

'Angling for position, moon lady?'

'Maybe,' she agreed. 'Why didn't you put all the usual clauses in that agreement? Why didn't you make it so that if I ever left you I'd end up with nothing?'

She stiffened when he took her arm. She moved into the lift ahead of him and when the doors slid closed she was facing him in the small, enclosed space and she felt a wave of panic.

'Are we going to be adversaries for the next fifty years?' he asked softly.

Staring Jonathan down was one thing, but in the lift there were mirrors all around reflecting their image. She felt overwhelmed by his nearness and her throat tightened. Fifty years. Fifty years with Jonathan.

'We're not going to be lovers,' she whispered.

'Friends,' he suggested. 'It would be exhausting living together if we had to keep fencing full-time.' He wasn't laughing now. He was serious and frowning and watching her the way he might watch an opponent in a chess game.

She smoothed her hands along the front of her suit jacket. She remembered Thursday afternoon on the beach, Jonathan standing between her and the wind and her hair blowing everywhere as she stood in bare feet in the sand and negotiated this crazy deal with him. Somehow it had been easier then.

'Will you call me "moon lady" forever?' she asked in a husky voice.

He leaned back against the wall of the lift and ran one hand through his hair. 'Probably.'

She couldn't stop him. She'd already asked him to stop and he still called her that name that had started one moonlit night fourteen years ago. 'Do you have something against Cynthia?' she asked wearily.

'It goes with the way you're wearing your hair today.'

Her hand went to the knot of hair at the back of her neck. 'I won't change my hair when I marry you,' she said. Married. Jonathan across the table from her. Sleeping in the same house. . .the same apartment. She wasn't sure where she would end up living but she'd agreed that it wouldn't be in her house. Now, in the confined space of the life, she realised that living under his roof would put her in his power, despite everything in that agreement.

'Elegance and inhibitions,' he said. 'That's your armour.' His smile grew and she felt tension mounting within herself. 'Don't get me wrong. It's an intriguing exterior, fascinating because the mask is almost perfect.' His gaze flicked from her hair down the length of her pale green suit. 'If it were white,' he mused, 'there probably wouldn't be a fleck of dust showing on that suit. But I remember how you look without the armour, moon lady.'

She fought the heat crawling up her throat and made herself hold his eyes. 'It's a bad deal for you, Jonathan. You want something you're not going to get. One day I'll clear that debt and then we'll be watching each other across the width of a courtroom because I'll divorce you then.'

She wanted to see tension in him, some sign of anger. But he was relaxed, listening and not bothered at all.

'You have to know I'll divorce you,' she said, and wondered whom she was trying to convince — Jonathan or herself. 'And you may say I don't learn but you're not very sharp either. You just signed a pre-nuptial agreement with a bride-price and no protection against my suing you for the shirt you're wearing, when I leave you.'

He laughed. 'You missed out, too. Why didn't you ask for an outrageous allowance? I'd have given it to you.'

She frowned and felt her fingers curling in on themselves. How the devil could she deal with a man who didn't even take money seriously? Yet he'd amassed millions since he was a young ruffian stealing apples from her father's trees. And he'd just got her promise on paper and created a debt she could never repay. Money given because he wanted her to marry him. He had to be crazy. He was getting nothing but a high-priced sham in exchange for his bride-price.

Two hours ago, while Jonathan was looking after some business in his eleventh-floor office in this same building, she'd gone across the street to the library. She'd wandered into the reference section and looked up 'bride-price' in the encyclopaedia. She didn't know why she did it, perhaps some urge to make sense of this crazy contract between her and Jonathan.

The encyclopaedia had said that the payment of a bride-price was common in pre-literate societies and almost universal in some areas of Africa. Assets paid by the groom to the bride's family. That fitted because Jonathan's money amounted to an indirect payment to Allan, the only family she had left. Different societies had different versions of what rights a man got in exchange for his payment of wealth, but they all agreed that he was entitled to sexual access—the one right Jonathan had *not* claimed in that contract.

They also agreed that in a divorce the bride-price was returned to the groom. She might vow to Jonathan that she would divorce him, but the reality was that she hadn't a chance in hell of finding enough money to pay back her bride-price.

This marriage would last as long as Jonathan wanted it.

The wedding was a civil ceremony held in the pent-house of Jonathan's Vancouver condominium. It terri-fied Cynthia.

She'd told herself that she would feel numb. She'd expected not to care. The size of the debt Allan owed to Garth Synerson had haunted her for weeks and she'd taken the only way out. She hadn't spent a lot of time thinking about the ceremony.

She thought she could handle the reality of daily life as Jonathan's wife. Hadn't she played the same arti-ficial role during her marriage to Eric? She'd withstood political lunches and charity balls and even television interviews. And all the time her relationship to Eric had been more that of brother and sister than man and wife.

A sham. A part she played. That was what marriage to Jonathan would be, just another part. But, standing in front of the commissioner with Jonathan at her side, she felt the panic begin and she wasn't sure why.

Perhaps because Allan was watching and he didn't approve.

She'd demanded of Jonathan that no one but the lawyer be privy to the truth of their marriage. If she was going to play this role it would only work if there was no one who could give her knowing glances. Especially not Allan, who must never know the price she'd paid to resolve his financial mess.

Playing the part with Allan had been unexpectedly difficult.

'You're *what*?' he'd demanded when she'd phoned him three days earlier. 'You can't marry Halley!'

'I want you at the wedding,' she'd said. 'And

Jonathan's picking up your note so please co-operate and come.'

Allan had been silent a long moment before he'd asked cautiously, 'Is that why you're marrying him? To pay off my note?'

She thought her laugh might have done justice to a great actress. 'I'm marrying him because he asked me. I've always had a thing about Jonathan.' It had scared her to hear her own voice making that statement. Jonathan had been her first wild, adolescent love but she'd spent years trying to hate him. Now she was standing beside him with the commissioner reading vows and she wasn't sure what she felt.

She couldn't forget the past.

Neither could Allan. The two men had met at the door of Jonathan's apartment like enemies only an hour ago. They'd stared at each other for a long moment and it was Allan's eyes that had dropped, which made no sense at all. She didn't understand how Jonathan could feel such anger against Allan when it should be the other way around. Allan's reaction didn't make sense either. Dropping his eyes. . .

The wedding. . .

'Do you want a double-ring ceremony?' Jonathan had asked on Tuesday, when he'd taken her shopping for a ring.

'No,' she'd said. They'd been at the entrance to an expensively tasteful jewellers. She'd stopped and said clearly and quietly, 'You're the one who's buying me. I didn't ask for any claim to you.'

Until that moment she'd thought nothing could shake his determination to let her barbs flow over him without reaction. But his eyes had flared and his face went hard so that she'd drawn back and pressed her lips closed, and for a full quarter of an hour she hadn't said a word to him.

He wanted her. He intended that in the end she would be entangled with him emotionally as well as legally. She was aware of that all week and slowly there grew in her the conviction that his desire to marry her was more than a resurrection of what he'd felt as he'd come towards her across Lacey's living-room all those years ago.

It was something darker than Jonathan felt for her now. She couldn't help feeling that it had something to do with the past, with her father's hatred for Jonathan and Allan's accident. With Allan watching the wedding-ceremony with visible tension and Jonathan's sister standing ten feet away glaring at her.

Cynthia stared at the ring that had just been placed on her finger. If only she understood how the past fitted together to make the present. Jonathan taking her father's apples when he was a boy. Jonathan and her father facing off when Jonathan was seventeen and her father caught him talking with the fourteen-year-old Cynthia. They'd hated each other at first sight, young Jonathan and Cynthia's autocratic father.

Her father's decree that she not see Jonathan Halley. Then that last summer. Love and betrayal.

After the accident Cynthia had left Canada and Jonathan himself had left Parkland. But years had passed and somehow he must always have determined to get what he hadn't been able to have back then. It didn't make sense because *he'd* sent her away, but it must be true. He'd bought her father's estate in Parkland. He'd made that comment the day of her father's funeral, as if he expected her to need his help. And when she'd gone to him he'd decided too quickly. In the space of minutes he'd made the offer of marriage.

Too fast, unless he'd always planned this as the final coup in an old war against her father. He'd bought both Allan and Cynthia with possession of that promissory note. She frowned because it didn't make sense that the man standing at her side should need to prove that he could have what he'd been forbidden by her father when he was a boy. None of it made sense, but it was the only explanation available because surely Jonathan was acting to a plan.

He kissed her when they were pronounced married. His lips on hers and she would have pulled away in an instinctive reaction except for the warning pressure of his hand on her back. So she endured the warm pressure of his mouth on hers and when he released her she could see his sister over his shoulder.

Alicia Halley hated her. They had never been friends but Cynthia hadn't thought there was hatred until today when Alicia greeted Cynthia.

'I don't like this,' Alicia had said in a grim hiss. 'You and your family have never been anything but trouble to Jonathan and I told him he's making a big mistake.' Jonathan had come up behind her then and Alicia had pressed her lips together into a thin line and shaken back curly black hair that was an echo of Jonathan's. Jonathan's older sister. Cynthia had never known her except casually to say hello to if they passed on the street in Parkland.

But she was her sister-in-law now and she had to make the best of it. As Jonathan released her both Allan and Alicia closed in. Deliberately Cynthia moved towards Alicia.

'Thank you for welcoming me to the family earlier,' she said quietly. She gave Alicia a brief kiss on the cheek. The older woman almost shuddered. Then she must have exchanged some meaningful glance with Jonathan because she managed a stiff smile.

'Are you going away for a honeymoon?' Alicia asked.

Jonathan's hand settled on Cynthia's shoulder in a

possessive caress. 'We're taking a few days away from both our jobs. Somewhere we're not likely to meet the Press. We've avoided the news-hounds so far, but you never know.'

A honeymoon. She frowned and told herself it was all right. He'd signed that contract, had agreed to its terms. Nothing would happen unless she actually *asked*. They would become lovers only at her request.

An hour of social torture followed. Alicia was frowning every time Cynthia looked at her. The commissioner accepted a drink from Jonathan and congratulated them with a surreptitious look of envy at the obvious wealth of Jonathan's apartment. Allan emptied his glass too fast and took another, watching Jonathan with a frown that was either apprehension or anger. Then suddenly Jonathan was saying smoothly to Alicia and the commissioner, 'You'll forgive us if we rush you out? We've a plane to catch.'

Allan got to his feet awkwardly with the others. 'I'll be off, too.'

'Not yet,' said Jonathan. 'We'll have a few words before you fly back to Toronto.' He said it casually enough but Allan's face paled.

Jonathan walked Alicia and the commissioner to the door. Cynthia had to go with them, to say good-bye and pretend again that it wasn't hatred in Alicia's eyes.

That left Allan. Jonathan's face was grim as he turned back to her brother. 'We'll talk in my study,' he said, and he led the way.

Allan followed more slowly, resting on his cane as if he was tired. Cynthia wanted to go with them. Why was Allan so frightened of Jonathan? Why was Jonathan angry with Allan when surely there should be a legacy of sympathy at the very least?

Cynthia was left alone in Jonathan's living-room

when the study door shut behind the two men. She walked to the window, staring out over a magnificent view of Vancouver's English Bay. Freighters and sailboats and behind her the closed door to Jonathan's office. Not a sound through that door. Jonathan had let her think that she had some control with that business of the contract. It was a farce, because he'd taken Allan into his office and her brother had been apprehensive while Jonathan looked grimly angry.

She might keep him out of her bed, but he was determined to rule her life. He'd told his sister they were going away together. A honeymoon hadn't been in the bargain but she'd agreed to play her role and she'd been the one to insist that no one know their marriage was a sham. So she was stuck with the honeymoon and she felt a crawling nausea well up because Jonathan wasn't going to take her someplace with people all around. He would get her alone and he'd have a seduction planned. He believed he could persuade her to do the asking—to beg him to come into her bed.

Never!

What was happening in that study? Jonathan had promised to tie Allan's hands financially and she supposed he was doing that right now. Then, once he'd finished with Allan, the game of their marriage would begin.

She stepped through the sliding doors to his large rooftop patio. A penthouse suite. She might have been on the most isolated island in the world because there weren't any taller buildings in sight. A helicopter flew past overhead. She supposed the pilot might look down on her but there wasn't anyone else.

This was where she would live when she was in Vancouver. Under Jonathan's roof. She moved slowly to the big Jacuzzi and wondered if she would ever use it. Not with Jonathan at home. There was something too intimate about the thought of sitting in that hot water with the whirlpool turned on and Jonathan close enough to wander out and imprison her with his eyes. Stars overhead and Jonathan——

She shivered and turned towards a swinging lounger just as Allan came through the patio doors. He stopped a few feet away from her and rested his weight on the cane.

'I've got the boot,' he said. His normally smooth sandy hair was slightly disarranged as if he'd run his hands through it. His face reflected exhaustion more than anything else.

She frowned at him. 'What did Jonathan do to you?'

'Do?' He shrugged. 'Did you figure he had me on the rack?'

She frowned and muttered, 'You're both the same. Evasive as hell. What did he say to you?'

'He gave me a lecture on investment and told me to get out and let the newly-weds have their privacy.' He grimaced. 'He made me feel a damned fool about Synerson.'

'What else?' she demanded, because there had to be more. That look on Allan's face. As if some weight had been lifted from his shoulders in that room. But he'd known for days that Jonathan was covering his promissory note, so what else was there?

'Man talk,' said Allan. 'Come see me out, will you?'

The door to Jonathan's study was open and they passed it together, Allan's gait uneven because of the cane. She kissed him at the door. 'You're sure you won't stay? You're welcome, you know.' She suspected that Jonathan wouldn't welcome Allan staying but she wouldn't let that stop her. If this was her home now she was damned well going to treat it as such. That included inviting her brother to stay the night.

'On your wedding night?' He laughed, and gave her a one-armed hug. 'I really wouldn't do that. Come visit when you get back to Toronto.'

Toronto, and another of Jonathan's residences. She hadn't asked him but she knew from that damned magazine article she'd read that he had places scattered all over the globe. Residences where she had no choice but to live now. A golden cage, and it spread too widely, covered too much ground.

The door closed behind Allan and she was alone with Jonathan Halley. Married and alone.

The office door was open. He was still in there. She went past it warily, not ready to face him, hoping he would stay in there finishing whatever business was keeping him. With luck a phone call would come and they'd tell him the foundation to the new hotel had cracked and he was urgently needed—or whatever kind of emergency it was that could draw him away from her.

She went back out to the patio. Back to the edge of that hot pool. She stood staring down at it and thought about taking off her nylons and stepping into the water so that just her feet and lower legs felt the hot, soothing power of the water.

She'd worn a belted mauve silk dress for the wedding. She supposed she should change before they went wherever it was they were going. Jonathan had had her luggage brought here on Monday and she'd slept here three nights already. Three nights under his roof, but he'd been on Vancouver Island supervising the work on the hotel.

'Make yourself free with the equipment in the study,' he'd said. 'It's going to be a couple of weeks before you can get back to Toronto.'

She hadn't asked why. She'd been moving in a numb acceptance of her fate ever since she signed that contract. A couple of weeks and perhaps she would have to give dinner parties and smile and pretend. . . and each night sleep in the room she'd slept in for the last three nights. It wasn't the master bedroom and although she'd used his computer and the fax machine in the office she hadn't opened the closed door to his bedroom. She didn't want to know what it looked like in there.

She'd phoned her office and received a fax of the latest drawings for the design of the day-care building for The Heights development. She'd stared at the drawings and thought about asking Jonathan because after all he was an architect and it was crazy to marry a man who had been described as one of the ten best architects in the world and not make use of his knowledge.

She hadn't asked him.

She crouched down by the water and trailed her fingers in it. Warm. Inviting.

'Go ahead,' his voice said.

She jumped and turned to face him. He was only inches away and she stepped back with a gasp. He reached out and caught her waist.

'You'll fall in,' he said. His voice was husky.

She brought her hands up to push him away but already she was too close to him. She could feel the agitated way her heart was hammering against his chest. 'Let go of me,' she whispered.

'Why?' She could feel his voice rumble against her breast. She began to tremble but she tilted her head back until she could meet his eyes. It was no use trying to fight Jonathan with lowered eyes.

'I don't want your arms around me,' she said clearly.

He studied her face for a long moment. 'Once you did.'

'I was a child then.'

'Hmm.' His mouth curved slightly. 'Perhaps not a woman. . .but not a child either.' His gaze caressed the length of her throat, paused where the crossed lapels of her dress revealed the beginning of her cleavage. 'If I let you go you might step back. You'd fall in. I don't know how that silk would survive the water.'

She pulled back in his arms, afraid to look down at herself in case her body reflected the images his words placed in her mind. Herself tumbled into the water and emerging wet, with the silk dress clinging intimately. His gaze hot on her and the revealing peaks of her nipples accentuated by wet silk.

'Let me go!'

He stepped back and she was carried with him. Then his arm slowly slid away from her waist. When it was gone she could still feel his touch.

'Where are you taking me?' Her voice was trembling. 'You told your sister we were going away but I warn you I — I'm not going to some isolated hideaway in the middle of nowhere. I won't be alone with you.'

His eyes widened and she realised that she was breathing too heavily, her confusion and distress reflected in her voice and the movement of her chest. He was watching and — damn the man! — he was turned on by her confusion, by the fact that his arm around her had made her. . .made her — uneasy.

'I won't be alone with you,' she repeated shakily. 'I refuse to——'

'We're alone now, moon lady.'

She didn't like the look on his face. As if things were going exactly as he planned. 'There's a city outside,' she said. 'If I had to get away from you I could——' Her voice faltered and she whispered, 'You wouldn't stop me, would you?' She swallowed panic. When a man promised not to consummate a relationship unless the woman asked — well, there were a lot of other things that might happen. Ways a man might touch a woman that probably counted as foreplay and she hadn't really thought of that when she'd made the bargain with him.

Jonathan had.

'Would you?' she asked. 'Would you. . .stop me?'

He slid one hand into the pocket of his dress trousers. 'You asked me to release you and I did.'

She gulped. 'Yes. . .but——'

'I would never use my strength against you.' His eyes were sober as he said, 'If you don't trust me you can leave now. I won't stop you.'

Her gaze flickered to the patio door behind him. She had only to go across the room and out the door to the main corridor. Down the lift from the penthouse to the ground floor.

'What about——?' She shivered and wrapped her arms around herself. 'What about Allan's note?' She looked back at him and his face was very still. She thought of a gambler waiting for the roulette wheel to stop and then the image flickered away.

'I don't intend to use any kind of coercion with you,' he said.

'That doesn't make sense,' she whispered. 'You— we made a deal. You bought that note—you—and I promised——'

He reached into his inside breast pocket and pulled out a folded sheaf of papers. Slowly he tore it across and dropped the torn pieces on to the patio floor.

She swallowed. 'Is that——?' She gestured towards the mess of torn paper on the floor. 'Is it——?'

'Two copies. You've got the only other copy.'

The contract they'd signed. Her eyes sought his. 'You're crazy,' she whispered. 'You should have left a copy in the lawyer's office.'

'So he told me.' He smiled wryly. 'Call it a gamble.'

His gaze flicked down to the torn papers, then back to her face. 'I'm gambling that I've got a better chance to make this into a real marriage if I untie the strings.'

She couldn't speak.

'You're free to leave,' he said softly. 'Any time you choose. I would never use my strength against you, moon lady. Not financially and not physically.'

CHAPTER FOUR

CYNTHIA glanced from Jonathan to the blue sky above them. 'Damn you,' she whispered.

He bent down and collected the scraps of paper into a crumpled ball. 'Changes things, doesn't it?'

She let out an explosive breath. 'Yes!'

He held the papers towards her. She turned and made a motion as if to ram her hands into her pockets but the dress had no pockets. She walked to the rail that had been built to prevent fools from tumbling thirty storeys to the ground.

'No,' she said grimly. 'It changes nothing.' She wrapped her arms around herself. She turned back to face him and she knew her posture had defensiveness written in every line, but even that didn't seem to matter. 'I signed a contract. You signed it too. Ripping it up makes no difference. I still owe you one hell of a pile of money and I can't pay.'

He shook his head and she saw one of his hands go into a fist but his voice was even and quiet. 'You owe me nothing. I would have covered that note even if you hadn't agreed to marry me.'

She'd known that the day they had signed the contract, hadn't let herself think about it because speculation would lead her to all sorts of dangerous possibilities. She swallowed and said, 'For Allan?' which was the only reason that could possibly leave her free, but he'd already denied any desire to help Allan. . .

'No. Not for Allan.'

She pulled her lower lip between her teeth. Her gaze

58

flickered from him to the open patio door behind him.
Past Jonathan and through the luxurious apartment
with its original paintings and Persian carpet. Out of
the door and into the lift.

'Go ahead,' he said. 'But I warn you, I'll follow you.
I'll be at your door and I'll be at the same parties you
go to. When you're invited to dinner I'll turn up sitting
beside you and when you buy property you'll find me
involved. And if the newsmen ask me questions, all I'll
say is that you're my wife, because whatever you decide
I'm giving you warning that I meant those vows we
exchanged today. Unless you can face me across a
divorce court and tell me and the world that our
differences are irreconcilable — unless you can do that,
I'm going to be in your life from here on.'

He didn't look happy about it and she shivered
because it must be some sort of compulsion he had.
But she had walked into this with her eyes open. She
thought he owed Allan but that didn't change anything.
Legally he owed Allan nothing and she could hardly
walk out on a moral obligation that measured more
than her total assets.

She thought of the day she had married Eric and that
scene afterwards in the study when she'd discovered
that her father's money was behind Eric's pursuit of
her. She felt as if she was going through the same play
again now, but upside-down, without knowing the
lines. Ten years ago she had been angry, but confident
that she could make a life for herself within the
parameters that her father and Eric had drawn around
her. Now she felt only confusion and danger. And she
was far too aware of the man facing her.

'I'm holding you to that contract,' she said in a voice
that trembled slightly. She lifted her chin. 'I haven't
torn up *my* copy.'

He smiled slightly. 'Will you hold it in front of you like armour?'

'Yes.' She wasn't returning his smile. 'And don't think I trust you an inch. This is strategy. You didn't tear that up out of generosity or—you did it because you—because——'

'Because I want you.' He spread his hands as if to show they held no hidden cards. 'No games, moon lady. The choice is yours. If you want to go by the contract that's what we'll do. If you want to leave. . .' a muscle flicked in his jaw '. . . then you're free to leave. Whatever happens, it's your choice.'

She shook her head. He'd freed her and left her no choice at all.

'I want a drink,' she said.

She hadn't realised the tension that had been in his body until he moved and it melted into lazy grace. 'Champagne?'

'No!' She followed him into the living-room. Her home, or one of them because Jonathan moved around a lot. She knew that from the article too, but she supposed soon she'd know at first hand. 'Mineral water,' she decided as he went behind the bar.

'Keeping a clear head?'

'Definitely.' If she was really staying with this man she'd better be certain never to have another drink.

Her choice, he'd said. Stay or face him across a divorce court. She would have to stand up in court and say—— She didn't know what she would have to say. She had never thought of divorce as something that could apply to her, but she wasn't at all certain she could handle a life at his side.

He put the cool glass of mineral water and ice into her hand.

'Thank you,' she said, forcing her voice to be steady.

He'd saved Allan and he'd saved her. It would be

easier if he'd held that contract up to her as a compulsion. Harder to be here when nothing but her own conscience stopped her from walking out of that door.

She took a long sip of fizzy water. 'Where are we going?' she asked carefully. 'You told Alicia we were going away.'

'Your choice.' He prowled to the mantel and stared at an abstract painting in reds and golds. The modern painting was oddly at home among the antiques in this room. 'I've got Eddie standing by with the jet at the airport. Name your destination.' He turned back to her with a slight smile on his lips. 'You wanted people, so we'd better not go to my place in the Mediterranean. It's on an island with a population of about forty and they mostly keep to themselves. So you choose, moon lady.'

Every time he called her 'moon lady' she felt a shiver down her spine and a wave of memory. 'We can't go back,' she said shakily, staring into her drink so that she wouldn't have to look at his eyes. 'You keep calling me "moon lady" but what happened fourteen years ago was an affair between two kids. It's over.'

She looked up and something in his black eyes made her shiver.

'If it's over,' he said quietly, 'then stop looking at me with the past in your eyes. If it's over let's start this marriage now. Today, with no past between us.'

She thought it would be impossible to do what he asked. Whenever she looked at him she saw the years of her teens and the brief light that was one week loving Jonathan. That week was irrevocably attached to the confusion and pain that followed.

'Why does Alicia hate me?'

He leaned one arm against the mantel and stared into the darkness of the empty fireplace. 'Ask her,' he suggested.

'You don't deny she hates me? You must know why.'

'There's no percentage in this.' He tossed his hair back with a jerk of his head. 'Leave it alone.'

She made a sound of frustration, 'I don't suppose you'd tell me what happened after Allan's accident? Why everything changed? Why the next morning when I ——' She gulped and whispered, 'Why *you* changed?'

He prowled towards her until they were only a touch apart, then he studied her as if he could read the thoughts from her mind.

'No,' he said finally. 'Leave it, Cynthia. You're not going to untangle our past. The future is all there is.'

She made a bitter sound that might have been a laugh. 'You say I'm free to walk out?'

'I won't stop you.'

But he would follow. He would turn up at dinner parties and he'd be tangled in her business deals. She lifted her glass and she wondered what he would do if she threw the contents into his face. It would be an outrageous thing to do. The sort of thing she had *never* done in all her life. She stared at the hard lines of his face and thought that if she turned hysterical she would be the only one to lose. Hysteria would win nothing against Jonathan's cool determination.

'You're all locked doors,' she said wearily. 'You say you want me. . .but the doors are all locked.'

'The doors to the past,' he said. 'There's only trouble in the past. Leave it where it belongs. Where do you want to go for our honeymoon?'

She sighed. 'Timbuktu,' she suggested, then she grimaced. 'I suppose your jet could take us there.'

'Definitely.' He was smiling, but only with his lips. 'Watch what you wish for.' He took the empty glass from her hand. 'Is that your choice?'

She grimaced. 'All my life people have made choices for me. Now you've given me a choice and the ironic thing is that I'm not free anyway.' Her eyes went to the door that would lead to freedom from him. False freedom.

'What stops you?'

'Conscience,' she said wryly. 'You may say I owe you nothing but I know differently.'

'And you'd feel free if I said the money was for Allan's sake?'

'Yes.'

He studied her for long seconds. 'And I wonder what would happen then?' he mused. He shrugged and lifted his glass to his lips. 'I've never lied to you yet, moon lady. I'm not going to start now. If you want to leave, then go. But I'm not adding to the misunderstandings between us now.'

'Or clearing the old ones up,' she said bitterly.

'No.' His voice was implacable. 'So are you going out that door? Or are we going away together?'

She drew in a long breath. 'We made a deal. I'm not quitting and I'm not running. But it's going to be a boring honeymoon.' She saw desire flicker in his eyes and she said resolutely, 'I'm holding you to that contract and I want separate rooms whenever we stay in a hotel.'

He ran his fingers through his hair and she saw laughter in his eyes. 'The newsmen will find that interesting when they catch up with the fact that we're married. Why don't we compromise on a suite?'

They decided to go to Cabo San Lucas because neither of them had ever been there and they thought the southern tip of the Mexican Baja was an unlikely place for gossip columnists. In fact, the media caught up with them before they left Canada. As they climbed out of the limousine at Vancouver Airport they came face to face with a couple who were obviously newsmen, one carrying a camera and the other with eyes that widened as if he had recognised either Jonathan or Cynthia.

It was all too likely that they'd been recognised, especially Jonathan, who seemed to make news wherever he went. Last year, in Nova Scotia, he had walked into an angry group of demonstrators picketing a conference centre he was building. She'd watched the incident on television news, holding her breath when Jonathan walked straight into the shouting crowd. Somehow, he had sorted out the leaders of the demonstration and they'd disappeared with Jonathan into one of those yellow and white trailers like the one where she'd found him a week ago in Parkland.

'We've got a reasonable compromise,' the environmentalist had said when the cameras caught him later. Jonathan had agreed and the next week there was another article in a leading financial publication. About Jonathan Halley—the man who built revolutionary structures on schedule, who built them better and stronger and more profitably than most of his competitors. The article had said that Jonathan generally put his own money in at the beginning and sold out for a profit a couple of years after the building was functioning as a luxury hotel or a revolutionary new theatre.

It had said that Jonathan dealt with problems and came out the winner because he knew how to compromise with labour unions and government while still getting what he wanted. He was described as a man for the twenty-first century, an environmentally conscious capitalist. The article had shown the revised plans for the conference centre on the east coast. It would adjoin a protected nesting ground for birds. Live cameras would be installed so that bird watchers could observe video displays of what went on behind the high fences. A world organisation for the preservation of endangered species had announced plans to hold their next major symposium in the new conference centre. Revolutionary, the article had said, and other developers would soon be forced to follow Halley's example of capitalism and environmentalism working hand in hand.

The reporter at the airport recognised Jonathan. Maybe he had read that article or he might even have written it.

'Mr Halley?' he called out. 'Is is true that you've invested in the Synerson project?'

Jonathan took Cynthia's arm and turned so that he was between her and the newsmen. He didn't stop walking but he smiled and said firmly, 'No business talk today. Ask me when I get back from my honeymoon.'

It distracted them effectively. The man with the camera raised it and Jonathan said, 'One picture, that's all.' His hand tightened on Cynthia's arm. She managed a smile as the camera flashed because she had a horrifying vision of herself in newsprint looking as if Jonathan was dragging her away against her will.

'Sudden, isn't it?' persisted the reporter. The photographer was frowning as if he thought he should be able to place Cynthia.

'Hardly.' Jonathan looked down at Cynthia and his lips curved as if at a cherished memory. 'Cynthia and I have known each other for years.'

'We met on my thirteenth birthday,' said Cynthia. She was amazed at how natural her voice sounded. Jonathan's touch was burning through her sleeve and she was talking as if this were a cocktail party.

'Dyson-Paige,' said the photographer. 'You're Cynthia Dyson-Paige. That Parkland development is going in on your old family estate.'

'We've a plane to catch,' said Jonathan firmly. He

grinned and added, 'We got married this afternoon. So
far as I know you're the first to know about it.'

'Thanks!' said the reporter and Cynthia heard the
camera flash going off again as they went through the
doors into the terminal.

'I thank you, too,' said Cynthia quietly.

Jonathan looked down at her with his brows lifted in
query.

'They knew somehow about the Synerson thing. But
you made it — make *us* seem very natural.'

He shrugged. 'You helped. You threw in the bit
about the birthday.'

'I'll get asked about that again if they print it.' She
grimaced. 'I'll end up having to tell them that Lacey
Wilkins's big brother pushed me into the mud in my
new dress and you got in a fight over it.'

'Over here,' he said, steering her away from the
ticket counters to an inconspicuous corridor. 'Will you
add that I got suspended from school for a week for
fighting?'

'Wouldn't do much for your reputation, would it?'
She couldn't help smiling, remembering how he'd
pulled her out of the mud and tried to clean the dirt off
her face with Kleenex while Lacey's brother wailed
that Jonathan had given him a bloody nose.

She looked back and the reporters were gone. For
good or ill, her marriage to Jonathan was public
knowledge now. Just as well they were escaping the
country for a few days. Back in Toronto the society
columnists would be scurrying to catch up with missed
news by morning. Here in Vancouver too because this
was Jonathan's home and developers in this part of the
world remembered her father.

After the confusion of the airport Jonathan's jet
seemed a haven of peace with soundproofed walls and
comfortable leather reclining seats. 'Get some sleep,'

Jonathan suggested when the doors closed and the pilot disappeared up front. 'Or read a book. It's been a long day.'

If it were a real marriage, she might spend the flight sitting at her husband's side, curled against him. He might look down at her and kiss her and they would both be yearning for the end of the journey, for the room waiting for them. . .the bed they would share.

She pushed at her hair and looked around the interior of the jet. Built for business. It had a desk at one end with what looked like a fax machine and telephone.

'Satellite telephone,' Jonathan said when she frowned at the equipment.

'Work while you fly,' she said idly. She sat down in a soft reclining chair near a window and picked up a book from a shelf beside the chair. She grimaced at the title and muttered, '*Stress factors in Concrete Structures*? This is supposed to relax me?'

He laughed. 'There are some thrillers on the shelf behind you. And magazines.'

She went back and frowned at the selection of books. Then she glanced at Jonathan and saw that he'd opened his briefcase and was sitting at the desk with a frown of concentration.

She wasn't going to be able to read but she picked up *The Russia House* by Le Carré and went back to the reclining chair with it. She found a lever on the side that freed the chair to turn. She adjusted it so that she was facing the window with Jonathan off to her left at the front of the plane. She would have to turn her head if she wanted to look at him.

The cabin was soundproofed enough that she could hear the rustle of papers from Jonathan. When he picked up the telephone she heard his voice, too. It was pitched low but if she strained she could hear that

he was checking on the delivery of trusses. Then
another call and he was speaking in Italian but she
didn't know enough of the language to understand
what he was saying.

'You speak Italian?' she asked when she heard him
hang up the receiver. 'I knew you spoke French but I
didn't know about Italian.'

'And German,' he said.

'Oh.' She managed not to fall into the temptation to
turn and look for the expression in his eyes. She could
sense that he was looking at her.

'Why don't you take your hair down, moon lady? It
can't be comfortable trying to relax with a knot of hair
pressing into the back of your neck.'

She smiled slightly because he made it sound almost
a torture instrument. 'My armour,' she said. 'I'll keep
it on.'

After a moment she felt her tension ease and she
knew he had turned back to his papers. She curled her
fingers tighter around the book and closed her eyes.
She heard the jets change to a louder pitch and
Jonathan's voice telling her to do up her seatbelt. She
felt for it without opening her eyes and when it was
done up she felt the jet moving.

She was aware of the sounds, the bumpy feel as they
went through the clouds. Then the quieter tones of the
engines as they levelled off somewhere up in the sky.
They would be in the air for five hours. She wondered
how she was going to get through seven days in a
luxury hotel with Jonathan when her nerves screamed
every time his hand brushed against her.

She had to pretend he was a stranger. A new
acquaintance. Forget about everything. The past was a
mess and the future was all there was. She frowned and
twisted in the chair. The sound of the jet droned on
and, as Jonathan's voice murmured in the background,

she drifted through a confused medley of memories and fantasies.

Jonathan slipping a ring on her finger earlier today. . . Alicia glaring at her with hatred. . . Allan looking uneasy. . .

Older memories. . . Jonathan reaching down a hand and her taking it. Being drawn into that first dance. . . further back. . . Jonathan holding her in his arms as she came to her senses after being thrown by the horse. . . Jonathan threading his fingers through her hair and speaking words that she couldn't make sense of. . .the sound of his voice stoking her nerve-endings and excitement crawling through her veins. . .

'Moon lady, you're grumbling in your sleep.'

Jonathan's voice. His touch on her arm and she dragged her eyes open.

She must have slept. She was filled with the dull lethargy she'd brought back from the place she'd been. Filled with the past.

'Where are we?' she whispered.

'Somewhere over Oregon.' His voice was gentle. There were two deep frown lines between his eyebrows. She studied them.

'What's wrong?' she asked huskily. 'Why are you frowning at me?'

'You're talking in your sleep.' He touched her hip and she felt the pressure of the seatbelt releasing.

'What are you doing?' she demanded weakly. His hands were in her hair now and she saw his lips part. If he kissed her she might go up in flames with those memories prowling through her veins. She jerked away but there was nowhere to go, only the back of the seat and Jonathan leaning over her and her heart thundering panic.

'Don't!'

'For God's sake, Cynthia!' His mouth tightened.

'You surely don't *sleep* with your hair up! I'm not spending the next four hours watching you frown in your sleep.' He fumbled with her hair and she felt the instant when he freed the clasp that anchored it.

'You don't have to watch,' she mumbled.

He laughed then, and said 'Go back to sleep,' and her eyes closed so that her world was Jonathan's hands in her hair, spreading it free, his voice murmuring, 'I always loved your hair, moon lady.'

Cynthia went to Lacey Wilkins's party because she was afraid of what would happen if she stayed home.

It had been a long summer on the estate at Parkland. Cynthia was sixteen and her brother Allan two years older. Allan was restless. He'd been in trouble all summer, sneaking into pubs and arranging parties on the beach with the wild crowd that Cynthia had been forbidden to speak to.

Allan had been forbidden to associate with them too, but he was in a state of constant rebellion. In August, an hour after their father left on a week long trip to Toronto, Allan exploded through her bedroom door with restless energy.

'I'm going to Lacey's party,' he announced.

'Dad won't like it,' Cynthia warned.

'He won't know,' said Allan. 'He's got no damned right to tell me where I can and can't go and who I can't see.' Her brother did a circuit of the room and suddenly swung back to announce, 'You'd better come too.'

'No way.' Lacey Wilkins had been Cynthia's friend until last year, when Lacey had started dating Blake, the leader of the crowd Cynthia's father forbade her to speak to.

'You have to come. The party's down at Qualicum. You know damned well the witch isn't going to give me the keys to your car. So how the hell am I to get there?'

The witch was Mrs Corveson, their father's resident housekeeper. She had their father's emergency telephone number. A call from her would bring Samuel Dyson home in a rage if either Cynthia or Allan got into what she termed 'trouble'.

Cynthia would have loved to find out what happened at one of those parties, but she wasn't courageous enough to risk her father's wrath. 'I'm not going,' she said. 'I'm going to watch a movie on television tonight.'

Allan frowned at her. 'Give me your keys, then.'

She came to her feet, breathing hard. 'Don't be a fool! If you get in trouble again —— She'll know the car is gone and she'll phone ——' Horrible images flashed into Cynthia's mind. A party, and of course there would be drinking. 'What if you get stopped by the police?'

Allan's driving licence had been revoked six months ago, and he'd been placed on probation after a third charge of driving while impaired. Cynthia knew that it was only the fact that their father had hired one of the best lawyers in the province that had kept Allan out of gaol. She couldn't believe he was crazy enough to consider driving with the threat of a probation violation hanging over his head.

He went to the door, throwing back, 'If you weren't such a coward it would be no problem. Tell the witch you're going to stay over at a girlfriend's and take the car.' He shrugged and grinned with the charm that had got her into trouble too often.

'Stay over! I'm not staying out all night!'

He came back into the room with his smile growing, as if he sensed that he was winning. 'Of course not, but you'll be back too late for the witch to be happy. She'll put a curfew of eleven on you, and what with the drive to Qualicum and back you won't be home until about one.'

Staying out after midnight had an appeal that made her nervous. 'But I wouldn't be able to come home! What would I do?'

He shrugged. 'We'll stay on the boat and you'll turn up bright-eyed and bushy-tailed just before lunch.'

'No. I'm not doing it.'

He sighed. 'All right, then.' He turned to go. His eyes flickered to her bag and he reached for it. She got to it before him and jerked it out of his reach.

'I know where the witch keeps the spare set of keys,' he said.

'You're not taking my car? You wouldn't—if you get caught——'

'How else can I get there?'

'Don't you have friends who can drive you?'

'Already gone. If the old man hadn't been so late leaving I'd have hitched a ride with Lacey's brother but——' He shrugged. 'Too late.'

She could see the next twenty-four hours in a horrified vision. He would take the keys and Mrs Corveson would place the call. Then the police would stop him and, the way Allan had been lately, Cynthia thought he would have been drinking. And if the shouting she'd heard through the walls when he got in trouble last time was right, then this time Allan would go to gaol.

'All right,' she said. She stood up and her mind went cold, as if, once having decided to do this crazy thing, there was no poing in being afraid. 'I've got to get changed. I can't wear this to the party.'

Allan prowled to her wardrobe and pulled out a silk shirtwaister in black and red swirls. It was dramatic and she'd only worn it once for a reception her father had taken them to in Paris, the year before.

Thank God no one at the party was going to be

talking to her father. In the silk dress she would be sure to be noticed!

'You'd better go,' she told Allan as they took the dress from the hanger. 'If you leave with me she'll think something's up.' Being a boy, under her father's weird rules Allan didn't have a curfew. Just rules, and right now both drinking and driving rated as capital offences for Allan. 'I'll pick you up at the gate-house,' she said.

Under the calmness she was scared. This was only the second time she'd sneaked out to a forbidden event. The first time had been for Allan, too. She'd been caught that time. She didn't intend to be caught again.

She went downstairs and checked that Mrs Corveson was watching television in her room. 'I'm thinking of going to spend the night at Debby's,' she announced.

'OK, dear,' said the elderly housekeeper. 'Have you called her?'

'Just doing it now,' she said, and she called Debby Fondyke with Mrs Corveson listening. 'Can I stay over?' she asked. Later she would call Debby back from outside the house and explain. Allan would think she was paranoid, but Cynthia had no desire to get into trouble. Allan did enough of that for both of them.

The scheme worked as if she had been meant to go to the party. When Cynthia set off with the red silk dress on under a light cotton coat she felt excitement welling up. She'd missed Lacey, and maybe Allan was right. Her father had the archaic idea that their social status and money meant that they had to live a restrictive life of his choosing. She wasn't about to rebel openly, but with the car purring and Allan waving to her from the gatehouse she thought maybe she would be a little more daring from now on.

Carefully, of course.

After she picked up Allan, she stopped at a pay-phone and straightened things out with Debby.

'My parents aren't home,' said Debby. 'They went over to Vancouver for the weekend. So have a good time and you're free to come back here to sleep when it's over.'

'Do you want to come?' she asked and from the open window of the car she heard Allan groan.

'She's a wet blanket! Don't invite her!'

But Debby's boyfriend was taking her out to the theatre that night. Debby promised to prime her house-keeper in the unlikely event that Mrs Corveson called. 'It's time you had a bit of fun,' she said and Cynthia's determination grew stronger.

'Let me drive,' said Allan when they cleared the town of Parkland.

'No way!' She glared at him. 'The only way we're doing this is with me at the wheel!'

He gave in, and muttered that she drove like a girl.

When she parked outside Lacey's summer cottage on the waterfront at Qualicum they could hear the music pounding through the sea air.

'Her parents can't be here,' said Cynthia.

Allan laughed.

It was louder inside. Lacey was wearing a slinky sheath dress that showed every curve of her body. With the music pounding in her ears and a boy she hadn't seen before prowling towards her, Cynthia grabbed Allan's arm.

'You'll stay with me, won't you?'

He didn't of course.

Cynthia evaded the tall predatory boy and found haven beside a girl she recognised from her last year's biology class. 'Great party!' said the girl.

Cynthia looked around and thought it was going to be a long night. She saw Allan with a bottle of beer in his hand. Someone shouted,'Hey, there's Denny with more booze!' as the door opened.

She had her car keys in her bag. Someone turned the music louder and Cynthia decided that she would leave soon. It wouldn't take long for the noise to pall and she could see the predatory boy getting ready to try another approach.

The door to the outside opened again. She turned to look. Then she stopped breathing because she knew now why she'd come. Not for Allan, but because Jonathan might turn up here.

Jonathan Halley had been her secret friend for three years. He'd defended her against Lacey's older brother the day they first met in the school grounds. A year later he'd picked her up after she was thrown from a horse and they'd talked under the apple tree. A month after that her father had caught her talking with Jonathan on a downtown Parkland street. He'd warned Jonathan to stay away from Cynthia that day.

Jonathan hadn't taken the warning seriously because whenever they ran across each other he still stopped to talk to her. A few months ago he'd stopped when she was sitting on a bench in the park feeling as if her life was hopeless. Of course, he hadn't known how miserable she'd been that day. She certainly hadn't told him. But they'd talked about the way the sailboat out in the harbour was tacking into the wind and how Jonathan's father had broken his leg in an accident in the bush. Then Jonathan had smiled in a way that made her heart stop and he'd asked if she would go out with him. It was two years since her father had warned him off, and maybe he'd thought the warning didn't apply any more.

'No,' she'd said. 'I can't.' Then she'd smiled nervously and added, 'I'm sorry.'

He'd smiled back and told her that he would try

again. Of course, she couldn't go out with him but he'd made her day brighter and she'd dreamed about him that night.

And he was here tonight, at Lacey's party. He stopped with the open door of Lacey's summer home still in his hand. She saw him look around the room as if to tabulate who was there. She had time to study the way his jeans fitted as if shaped to him, the way his white cotton shirt made a sharp contrast over the denim. The top two buttons of the shirt were unbuttoned and she could see a black tangle of hair. He was frowning, and she had the panicked thought that he might turn and leave.

Then his eyes found hers.

A couple locked in an intense embrace danced between her and Jonathan. When she saw him again he was halfway across the room. Someone called his name and he didn't turn to look, just lifted his eyes on her in a way that made her aware of the silk folds of her skirt falling away from her crossed legs.

He held his hand out towards her. 'Moon lady, you'd better dance with me,' he said. Her hand rose to his and he slowly pulled her to her feet. They stood like that, staring at each other. It was the first time she'd stood head to head with him. She looked most boys in the eye but she had to tilt her head back to lock eyes with Jonathan. She swallowed at what she saw in his black eyes. 'It's time we did something about this,' he said and he drew her towards the open patio door.

She didn't talk until they were outside on the beach. 'You said we should dance,' she breathed then. She stared down at his hand and it was still locked on hers. She let her eyes take the long journey up his arm. The white sleeves were rolled up to expose muscular forearms. She knew he worked at logging with his father during the summer and wondered if it was using a chain-saw that gave him muscles like that. Her brother's arms were light and fragile by comparison.

'We're not dancing in there,' he said. He still held her hand but he made no move to take her into his arms. 'It's a jungle in there.'

Out here it was moonlight and dreams, the music softened by distance.

'Why did you call me moon lady?'

He grinned and in the moonlight his face looked older, both harsh and amused at the same time. 'Cynthia sounds like someone who wears pearls and gets her picture on the society page,' he said.

She frowned. She was wearing pearls tonight, and last month in Vancouver her picture had been on the society page after she attended Allison Weighton-Price's sixteenth birthday party at the Royal Vancouver Yacht Club.

He brushed her cheek lightly with one hand. 'Cynthia is also a name for a Greek moon goddess. I'd rather think of you as the moon lady.'

'Do you think of me?' she asked on a breath.

He was holding her hand and his thumb was caressing the back of her fingers. At Allison's birthday party a well-bred young man had caught her behind the refreshments stand and stolen a kiss. She wondered if Jonathan meant to kiss her and she decided that if he did she wouldn't fight the way she had at Allison's party.

'My father doesn't want me to talk to you,' she said. She felt mortified as the words came out. He would think her too young, too sheltered.

'Yes,' he said. 'I remember. Do you always choose the friends your father wants for you?'

She shook her head. 'Not always,' she said. Until now she had, but tonight that would change.

He let her hand go and held his arms out for her.

She put one hand on his shoulder and the other into his. His arms were hard and gentle at the same time. He didn't hold her too tightly the way some boys did but when they moved over the sand she found her body nestling against his and his mouth against her ear.

Magic. Moonlight and Jonathan and the music. She closed her eyes and he brought her gently closer. Her head was against his chest and he murmured against her hair, 'Can we take this down?'

She stared up at him with her body still swaying to the music.

He murmured, 'I want to kiss you, moon lady, but I want your hair down when I do it. I want to see the moonlight on your hair.'

She stood immobilised by his spell as his hands rummaged in her hair. Then it all came tumbling down and he breathed something she couldn't catch and drew her mouth into his, his hands in her hair and his lips parted.

She melted when his lips found hers. That was what it felt like, melting like chocolate with the flame under it, his hands in her hair moving softly and his mouth gentle so that there was nothing to pull away from but magic.

When he murmured, 'Open your mouth for me,' she closed her eyes and let her lips part while Jonathan taught her what kissing was really about, there on the beach at Qualicum.

CHAPTER FIVE

THE beach at Cabo San Lucas was only a breath away from their suite. Both bedrooms and the sitting-room opened on to a tiled patio. Cynthia could step outside her bedroom and lean against the marble balustrade of the patio, staring at the ocean. Sailing ships at anchor off the right. Further right a fleet of marlin fishing boats moored close to the beach. Nothing but boats between that beach and the beginning of Antarctica.

Watching the empty ocean southwards, Cynthia felt as if she was standing in a protected circle of peace. A world that held only herself and Jonathan.

The hotel was a white luxury palace sprawled along the beach east of Cabo San Lucas, away from the concentration of tourists. Three steps down from the patio she could walk on pure white sand and sometimes it seemed to Cynthia that the beach was theirs alone.

When they checked into the hotel on their wedding night, the manager showed them to the suite and personally directed the luggage into the larger of the two bedrooms. Cynthia stood frozen in the sitting-room while Jonathan followed the manager.

Both their suitcases had gone into that master bedroom.

And Jonathan had torn up the contract between them.

She turned away and fled through the open patio doors with her heart pounding in sudden panic. She could hear their voices, could feel her nerves crawling with tension each time her ears responded to the rumble of Jonathan's voice. Then the manager threw open the glass doors from the big bedroom and both men stepped out.

Her husband.

This was no marriage of convenience, not from his point of view. *He* wanted her. And Jonathan had a way of getting the things he wanted. She stared across the ceramic tiles, her gaze pulled to his eyes. Once the manager left them alone, what was there to stop Jonathan taking what he wanted?

Only *her* will.

What would happen if his lips possessed hers while his hands explored the softness of her woman's curves?

The manager said something in heavily accented English. He smiled at her and she forced herself to smile back. She didn't know what he'd said but he was leaving now. She saw Jonathan slip a banknote into his hand. In a moment she would be completely alone with the man she'd married.

She turned away and looked rigidly at the ocean.

Jonathan would come to her now. He wouldn't have to force her. He had other weapons. Her memories could betray her too easily and Jonathan wouldn't be above using an advantage like that. He was already using it. He kept calling her 'moon lady' and that was nothing more than a way to bring the past alive.

Only sounds from behind her. Jonathan's footsteps. Then his voice.

'Cynthia, I'm going down to check about a rental car.'

'OK,' she said. Her breath drained out. She didn't turn to look at him.

She heard the door close behind him and wondered what on earth would be the shape of her future. Living under Jonathan's roof, and it couldn't go on forever without something shattering. Every beat of her heart told her that this man was even more dangerous to her than the boy he'd once been.

She explored the suite while he was gone. He had left her suitcase in the room with the king-size bed. He'd moved his own bag into the smaller bedroom with its twin beds. That should reassure her but it only reminded her of the terms of that contract.

He marriage would be consummated only at *her* request. If she wished, she could hold the contract in front of herself like a shield.

That big bed with its luxurious hand-woven spread. A bed meant for two. . . She had never shared a bed with Jonathan but there was a time when she'd dreamed of what it would be like to lie naked in his arms. And once——

The image wouldn't leave her.

Even later, when he returned from renting the car, she couldn't meet his eyes. She stood at the open patio door in the sitting-room and looked at the dark ocean.

'I'm tired,' she said. 'I think I'll——' Go to bed. She swallowed and amended that to, 'I'll turn in.'

'Goodnight,' was all he said.

She didn't look at him as she walked too quickly into that big bedroom. But later, staring at the moonlight flowing through the window, her old dreams seemed pale with the knowledge that Jonathan was only a quiet call away.

Was he sleeping?

The only safety she had was that she couldn't imagine *inviting* Jonathan, saying out loud that she wanted him to make love to her. Her pulse beat with heavy intensity. She was alone and awake and too aware. It was a long time before she could sleep.

The next morning over breakfast, she couldn't meet his eyes without remembering the restless heat of her broken sleep.

She had asked him to take her somewhere with other people, but unless they went into the town there weren't many. After breakfast they took the rental car into town. Jonathan strolled through the market at her side while she picked out light cotton clothing for the beach.

She deliberately chose loose T-shirts rather than the selection of imported brief halters. Even when she picked up white canvas shorts and a matching shirt with 'Cabo San Lucas' embroidered on it, she took a size larger than she would normally. She didn't want to expose suggestive surves. She was determined to do nothing that Jonathan might take as an invitation, especially with the memory of last night pulsing in her veins. Lying alone in tangled bedclothes with her senses reaching for the sound of his breathing, her body aching to hear his footfall coming close.

When she was sixteen, she'd been infatuated with him, had trusted him as she had never trusted anyone before. She'd thought it was the end of the world when he'd rejected her, but now the memory of her young passion felt tame in the shadow of the emotions of last night.

If she let herself. . .

She added a gauzy peach-coloured dress with a loose top and drifting skirt. It had been warm the night before. The dress would be cool in the evening and she could wear it to dinner and even dancing. Although it was attractive, it masked her curves with drifting gauze.

When Jonathan reached for his credit card to pay for her clothes, she shook her head. 'My clothes,' she said. 'I'm buying.'

'A matter of principle?' he asked, amused.

'Yes,' she said although she knew it was ridiculous to get her back up over a few pesos. Jonathan had flown her here in his corporate jet. He was paying the hotel and that miserable debt of Allan's. Logically, an armful of clothes made no difference, but the thought of wearing fabric he'd paid against her skin——There were too many forced intimacies already. She wasn't adding to them.

She pushed her credit card across the counter to the merchant.

The Mexican responded with an incomprehensible flood of Spanish.

'He's saying there's a surcharge on the credit card,' Jonathan said. 'I've got pesos to cover this. You can owe me.'

'I owe you enough,' she muttered to Jonathan. She turned away from him and nodded to the merchant.

After dinner that evening, when the Mexican musicians began to play soft Latin music, Jonathan put his glass of *cerveza* down. 'Dance?' he asked.

She had been expecting the invitation, had known he would use every opportunity to touch her, to pursue his stated intention of making their marriage a real one. His eyes were on her hands and she realised that she had been softly tapping one finger to the music. She stilled her hand but the heat didn't leave his dark gaze.

'No,' she said. 'I don't want to dance.' But she could feel his spell on her. If he stood and reached for her, nothing would stop her going into his arms to the beat of the Latin music.

'Then let's go for a walk on the beach before we turn in.'

She dared not let her eyes seek his. A walk and then. . .'Turning in' brought to mind the two bedrooms of their suite, separated by only the silent luxury of the sitting-room. In the dark warmth of a tropical night anything might happen.

* * *

They had the beach to themselves. Cynthia could hear the music still, its passionate beat blending with the black of the ocean under the glow of moonlight.

She walked slowly down towards the water and slipped her sandals off. She'd gone bare-legged in the warmth of the evening. Now she held the sandals in one hand and walked into the water with the awareness that Jonathan's eyes were watching her.

'You should live on the beach,' he said quietly. 'The water pulls you like a magnet.'

She walked along the shore with the water lapping just above her ankles. Jonathan kept pace on the sand. When she glanced at him she saw his hands in his pockets, his body moving with that lazy grace she would have recognised anywhere. She studied him in flashes from under lowered eyelashes.

'I thought you didn't speak Spanish?' she said. 'You understood the merchant about the credit card today.'

'I know a few words.' He shrugged. 'Between Italian and French I guessed the rest.'

She dug her toe into the wet sand. The water was unbelievably still. 'I should take you with me next time I go to Paris. After all those years of studying French I still——'

'Relax,' he suggested gently.

She stopped abruptly. 'I can't,' she whispered. He was uphill from her on the beach. She was standing in the water, the ocean a trap and Jonathan standing between her and freedom. 'I can't forget that you want—want. . .'

'That I want to make love to you?'

'Yes.'

His shoulders made a restless motion. 'Why is that a problem? It's your choice, after all. You don't have to say yes.'

'You're a man who has a hell of a record for getting

what you want. Have you ever lost anything that mattered to you?' He didn't answer and she thought the losses had all been ones he could walk away from. 'So it scares me,' she said raggedly. 'You scare me.'

The moon had to be growing brighter as she spoke. His shape was sharp in her vision now. The long strength of him and his face sculptured hard by light from the sky.

'Why should you fear me? You know I wouldn't force you.' He sounded so quietly reasonable. This was the way he must have spoken to that crowd of angry environmentalists.

She shook her head and the hair at the back of her neck seemed a weight pulling on her scalp painfully. 'You're too damned experienced and—I'm not. You hurt me once. And I—and——'

And she might say yes. The old spell was still there but it was worse now. He had new strength and a power that came from the years that had gone between.

'Would it be so terrible?' he asked quietly. 'We're married. I want you. If you're honest, you'd admit that you want me, too. If you invited me into your bed. . . His silence drew a graphic image of their bodies tangled in that big bed. 'Who would be hurt by it?'

She could be hurt. Terribly. 'And if I don't?' she breathed. 'Who would be hurt then?'

He lifted his head and she saw the slight smile curve his lips. Even in moonlight she recognised the emotion in him.

'You like a challenge,' she said. 'You enjoy the chase. Is that why you wanted me? Because the last time—when we were kids you didn't—we didn't actually——'

'We came damned close.' His low voice made her face flame.

She bent her head and walked rapidly along the

water's edge. 'How did you get from that logging company in Parkland to where you are now?' she asked wildly.

'The usual way.' She stole a glance and he was watching the sea now. Then he turned slightly and their gazes clung together even though it was only moonlight. 'University,' he said. 'This and that.'

'No details?'

'The details are too boring,'he said.

'I doubt that.' He'd been a logger and a student when she'd left for Switzerland, cutting trees to finance his university education. Then, somehow, he'd turned into the man who started projects, who'd built an empire of his own. He'd done all that on his own. Certainly his father hadn't left more than maybe a small insurance policy when he'd died as a result of that accident in the bush.

'What about you?' he asked. 'Your father made you vice-president of Dyson Holdings when you were only twenty-three. Was that what you wanted?'

'Yes,' she said. Had he read articles about her in the same way that she'd followed the public trace of Jonathan Halley?

'I didn't think the old bastard would share his empire with anyone.'

The sharpness in his voice brought back memories of the way her father had hated Jonathan. Of the feud that had started with a dispute over logging rights between their fathers.

'He didn't want to. I forced him.'

For a moment it seemed as if she could hear Jonathan's breathing in the stillness. 'Things must have changed after you left for Switzerland,' he said finally.

'Everything changed.' She bent and scooped up a handful of water. When she touched her lips to it, the sea tasted wild and salty in her mouth. 'Switzerland

changed me. Those years away from home—I learned
to be independent.'

Lonely years at first. She had missed Jonathan and
her brother achingly. When that had faded she was left
isolated from home in a strange way that felt almost
safe.

'You never came back to Parkland.'

'No.' She hadn't been back to the Parkland estate
until last week, looking for Jonathan. 'I didn't come
back from Europe until I married Eric. I wasn't even
home for holidays. And when I did return things were
different. I used to be afraid of Dad's rages, but when
I came back—I was older. Married. I—he'd lost the
power to frighten me.'

'There was a time when I'd have liked to kill him.'

Somehow his words had more power for being
quietly spoken. She wrapped her arms around her
midriff and admitted softly, 'It helped back then,
knowing you were angry. For me.'

She saw the shadow of his arm moving in an angry
gesture. 'There was damned little I could do until——'
He broke off with an explosive sound and said grimly,
'Enough of the past, moon lady. We have to leave it
behind us.'

She thought of Jonathan as she had once known him.
Of the accident that seemed to mark the change of
everything. Her distance from her own family. Allan's
injury. Jonathan's eyes turning cold, losing the tenderness she'd once found there.

'I can't forget,' she whispered. She turned away from
him and looked at the moon.

If they couldn't sweep away the mysteries that
shadowed their past, Jonathan would never win what
he wanted from her. A real marriage.

* * *

There was a young Mexican girl on the beach when Cynthia went down the next morning. She had woken early after a restless sleep, had dressed in shorts and the white canvas top. She'd gone into the sitting-room and had seen the door to Jonathan's bedroom standing open.

An invitation if she succumbed to temptation in the night?

No, he didn't expect to win that easily. But the open door *was* a message, reminding her that she was the one who closed doors between them. But it was Jonathan who had closed himself against her years ago when she'd needed him desperately. And now he wanted her to leave the past behind. To forget.

She'd walked down to the water in bare feet, knowing that he would wake soon and follow her. She saw the young Mexican girl sitting a couple of feet from the water constructing a sand-castle. The girl jumped up and faced Cynthia with a guilty look on her face.

She was about ten or eleven, and speechless.

'Hello,' said Cynthia carefully. 'Do you—*habla inglés*? Do you speak English?'

'Yes.' She smiled shyly. 'We live down there,' she added, and gestured towards the sprawling house on the point. Her English was pleasantly accented. 'My father is the hotel manager.' She looked around uneasily. 'I'm not supposed to bother guests.'

'I'm not bothered.' Cynthia dropped down beside her on the sand. 'What are you building?'

The girl's name was Maria and she was building a castle. She grinned when Cynthia suggested she might want help in the construction and the two sand-builders were soon intensely occupied in the construction of a somewhat original medieval castle.

When Cynthia looked up and saw Jonathan standing

beside them, the castle had grown very complex. He was smiling down at her and she grinned back.

'Heavy construction here,' she said.

'You're about to be swamped,' he warned.

She turned and saw that the tide had risen almost to their walls. Maria was staring at Jonathan with a mixture of curiosity and alarm.

'Maria, this is Jonathan. He builds castles all the time, but I'm not sure if he can save us from the ocean.'

'Hi, Maria,' said Jonathan easily. He crouched down to study the castle.

The girl smiled shyly, then glanced up at the hotel. 'I have to go,' she said on a rush. 'I'm not supposed to bother guests.' But she grinned as if the rule had been broken before and would be again without terrible repercussions.

'See you later,' said Cynthia.

'Sure! *Adios*!' The girl ran away along the sand towards the house on the point, turning back to wave before she disappeared.

'Interesting creature,' said Jonathan. He reached over and used his fingers to make a doorway in an interior wall.

'Hey! No modifications without the builder's approval!'

'Sorry.' He was smiling. 'But without the doorway you'd have to walk all the way around the castle to get into that room.'

She pushed her hand through her hair. Her fingers tangled in the knot of hair at her nape.

'Take it down,' he said. 'Let it free.'

She couldn't look away from his eyes.

'Wouldn't it feel better blowing free?'

She broke their locked gazes. 'I don't have a pocket to put the clasp in,' she said breathlessly.

'I do.'

As if under compulsion, she reached up and slowly unfastened the clasp. He held his hand out and she gave it to him, then she felt in her hair for the pins and handed them to him. As her hair blew free she said, 'It'll tangle if I don't tie it back.'

'I'll brush it out for you later,' he offered.

She stared down at the castle and touched one wall with her hand as if to assure herself it was still there. She fought the image of Jonathan brushing her hair with slow, sensuous strokes.

'Rather a modern-looking castle,' Jonathan commented. 'At least this end of it.'

'You won't tell Maria, will you? I was hazy on the details of medieval castles. This part of it is really the plan for a day-care and community centre in a subdivision near Toronto.'

'The Heights?'

She frowned and her hand clenched. 'How did you know about it?'

'Word gets around.' He was crouched on the other side of the castle, studying the walls of sand.

'Have you always kept track of me?' she asked.

'Yes. Why didn't you and McAulisson have children?'

She picked up a handful of sand and carefully placed it on top of an eroding wall. 'Maybe we didn't want them.' She spoke slowly, very deliberately.

'I don't know about him,' he said gently. 'But you wanted children.'

'You can't know.'

He gestured in the direction Maria had disappeared. 'I watched you with her. And I remember you telling me years ago how you wanted your own home, your own children.' He gestured to the castle. 'And whose idea was the day-care complex for The Heights?'

'Mine.' She shifted restlessly. 'But you already knew that, didn't you?'

'Yes.'

She piled more wet sand on the eroding wall but it was a losing battle. 'You put that business in the contract about if I — if there was a child. Was that part of your plan?' Even if he seduced her into the sort of madness where she begged him to love her, there would be no child. 'Is that how you planned to trap me?' she demanded, her voice rising. 'To make love to me and make me pregnant and——'

'I tore up the contract, Cynthia.'

'I didn't.' She pushed her hand through the sand wall and a room caved in on itself. 'You knew I wouldn't.' As always when she most wanted to read Jonathan's expression, there were no clues in his face to his real feelings.

He laughed with other men over coffee in construction trailers. He looked gentle and patient when he crouched down to talk to a young Mexican girl. But she knew another Jonathan, the man whose smiles died when she challenged him. The man who changed from loving tenderness to cold rejection in the space of one single night.

She wondered what either of them could win in this crazy relationship. He wanted her, but he looked grim now. As grim as he'd looked that morning on his front porch. And she——

She'd only married him because of Allan.

He reached down and pushed the sand against the place where she'd destroyed a wall. She stared at it and thought wildly that of course he would try to stop the wall crumbling. Jonathan Halley was a builder, not a destroyer. But he had torn up a contract that she'd thought made her safe enough to marry him. Torn it

up while he seemed willing to allow her to hold him to
its terms.

'If you wanted children from me,' she said in a voice
without expression, 'then you've got a poor bargain.'
She reached out one hand as if to destroy the wall
again but she couldn't do it. She clenched her fingers
and closed her eyes. A gust of wind blew her hair
across her face.

'Have I?' His voice told her nothing. She didn't let
herself open her eyes to look into his face.

She dragged in salty warm air and scooped the hair
away from her face with one hand. 'I had tests. The
doctors said I'd probably never conceive.' She glared
up at him. 'A thousand to one against my ever becom-
ing pregnant. That's what they told me.'

He was frowning, his eyes narrowed. 'I'm sorry,' he
said.

'I wasn't going to tell you that. But you see even
if——' She made an angry sound and muttered, 'You
don't get a very good deal for your money. There
won't be a child, Jonathan. If you wanted an heir——'

He reached across the crumbling castle and stopped
her voice with his fingers under her chin. He pressed
upwards until her eyes fluttered wide open to stare into
his. 'What do you think this is?' he asked gently. 'What
do you think I am?'

'I don't know,' she whispered. His eyes weren't quite
pure black. She'd never been this close, staring into his
eyes in broad daylight. The black contained golden
flecks of anger.

'I didn't marry you to get a child.' His words were
slow and flat so that she couldn't mistake them. 'I'm
sorry you can't conceive. I can see it's important to
you. But I'm not hung up on blood-lines and if I don't
have an heir to hand my assets on to when I die I won't
lose any sleep.'

Her eyes widened at the anger in his voice.

'On the other hand, we could always adopt,' he said. 'But don't attribute a bunch of stupid garbage to me about blood-lines and getting a child on you.' He took his hand away from her chin and stood abruptly. 'This isn't a breeding operation.'

'Jonathan——' She shook her head. 'I'm sorry. I wasn't trying to make you angry.'

'Yes, you were, moon lady.' His mouth twisted wryly. 'You always take a dig when I get too close.'

'I——' She had a horrible feeling that he was right.

'Defences,' he said. He smiled slightly. 'I wouldn't worry. I expect I can take more punishment than you're capable of dishing out.'

'I don't understand you,' she said soberly.

'No, I know you don't.

'You don't make it easy.'

He grinned at that. 'Is it supposed to be easy?'

'I don't know!' How could it be easy when they'd gone through a wedding-ceremony for such crazy motives? When she sometimes felt as if she'd had no choice, and at other times she felt she'd done something truly insane?

'It'll work out,' he said with quiet confidence.

She sighed and stood up, staring down at the castle. The outer wall was being eaten away by the ocean as she watched. 'Does everything work out for you?' She flung out a hand and muttered, 'Please don't answer. It was a stupid question. I just——'

'What about breakfast?' he suggested. He slid one hand into the pocket of his shorts. 'Then a trip out to sea for some whale-watching?'

She gulped and bit her lip. She had to ask.

'Jonathan, did you expect that we'd have children?'

'I thought it a possibility or I wouldn't have put it in that damned contract.'

She felt a wave of disappointment. Crazy to think he would say that he wanted only her, that he loved her so much nothing else mattered. She didn't believe in that kind of overwhelming love.

'Do you want a divorce?' she asked.

He had both hands in the pockets of his shorts. He wasn't looking at her but at the eroding ruins of the sand-castle. She wondered what she had come to that she could ache for him to say things he hadn't even whispered. She should be wild to get back to her own world, to Toronto and Dyson Holdings and The Heights subdivision that needed final plans approved.

She wanted to stay with Jonathan.

It was crazy. It wasn't even a marriage. It could never work between them. She would never be able to forget that once, years ago, he had pushed her away as if he hated her. So why did the crazy dreamer inside her yearn to be his wife? A real wife, with love and the kind of trust they could never build between them.

Oh, God! She was losing it. And if he saw, if he realised how vulnerable she was to him — if he ever knew that she loved him and had always loved him —

'Do you?' she whispered. 'Do you want a divorce?'

Why in God's name had she asked the question? Jonathan wouldn't lie. There might be things he would keep to himself until he died, but she believed he would never lie to her.

He drew a long breath that terrified her. Then he reached out his hand and grasped her arm. She felt as if she was being pulled into a hurricane.

'Moon lady,' he said grimly, 'don't you think it's time you stopped worrying about all the things we can't change and concentrate on where we are right now? You and I. Here.'

CHAPTER SIX

CYNTHIA gasped when the big whale surfaced and rolled only yards away from the boat. Jonathan pulled her back against him so that she was safe in his grasp with the breathless magic of the big mammal rolling just out of their reach.

She felt Jonathan's face moving against her hair, his voice murmuring, 'I love the smell of you.' The captain of the chartered boat couldn't possibly have heard, but Cynthia shivered and remembered how once his touch had stroked the barrier of clothing away. How she'd felt she might die just from the breathless magic of him.

The captain turned towards the shore and Jonathan guided her to a seat. Just a light touch of her arm, but once she had met his eyes boldly and now she could feel her lashes dropping because there was too much she needed to hide.

Eyes could issue invitations as easily as lips.

If she invited Jonathan into her bed she was lost. She would drown in him and when they got back to the real world he would turn away. She would be his wife and he would be. . . her life.

She tucked a strand of hair behind her ear and looked out over the endless ocean. When she could feel that his eyes had left her, she sneaked a glance and it was a picture she would have forever. Jonathan staring out to sea, his mouth straight as if there might have been a frown a moment ago. The clean, hard lines of his face and just a hint of the crease that could appear beside his mouth if he smiled. Dark brows above eyes that would show black if he looked at her now. Wild black hair tumbled by the wind.

She knew how he won those skirmishes with environmentalists and governments. Patience and iron determination and that instinct for the moment when an advance could not be rebuffed. Like this morning, when he had stopped the car at the market on their way to Cabo San Lucas's harbour where the charter boat awaited them.

'I'll be only a moment,' he'd said to her. He'd smiled with a hint of mischief in his eyes, a look she remembered from a younger Jonathan stealing apples from the big tree on her family's estate.

He'd returned minutes later with silky fabric streaming from one hand. He'd spread an assortment of scarves over her legs, a medley of red and black and smoky green.

'Which one?' he'd demanded.

She'd touched a blue scarf and it was silk, soft and elusive on her fingers.

'Turn a bit,' Jonathan had said and his hands had sought her hair.

'Jonathan! What are you doing?' she'd whispered. With his hands caressing her scalp and her hair tumbling everywhere it had felt almost as if he was undressing her. She'd reached up and grasped her hair and pulled it together at the back and his fingers had trailed away from her scalp with a light caress across her cheek.

He'd picked up a swirl of red and black silk. 'This one?' he'd asked.

She'd had a picture of an exotic dancer with a flaming red flower in her hair. Of Jonathan watching and she was the dancer, a slow seduction of music and erotic magic.

'The blue,' she'd said breathlessly. She'd grasped it

and it had slipped out of her fingers and into his. Then he'd reached and gathered her hair together, tying the scarf at the nape of her neck, so that when she moved her head she could feel the drifting sensation of her hair down her back.

'Much better,' he'd said. 'The whales will be enchanted.'

Every time the length of her hair down her back caught between them, every time his gaze drifted to it and she saw the flash of satisfaction in his eyes, she was aware of how easy it would be for him to pull the scarf away and send her hair free and wild. The image was strong, too graphic. Once, long ago, he'd come so close to making love to her that whenever she thought of a man and woman together it was Jonathan that she remembered. And in that memory her hair was wild and free and he'd made it that way.

She'd buried that memory for years, but it was always waiting for a weak moment. All the time Jonathan had lain waiting in her heart. Jonathan who wanted her. But he'd wanted her before and she'd called it love then. Until the end, when he'd torn her heart without even hesitating.

That night for dinner she wore the peach-coloured Mexican dress. It was loose and cool, modest over the bodice, gauzy cotton draping in folds down her back so that the movement of air cooled the flesh of her upper back.

She stared at her reflection in the mirror as she brushed the sea tangles out of her hair. When she reached for the pins, she paused. Jonathan's eyes would narrow if she came out with her hair dressed up. Before the evening was over he would find some way to send her hair tumbling down.

Her hand went to the jumble of silk scarves on the

dressing-table, but the colours were wrong for the dress. She picked up the brush again and slowly pulled it through her dark hair until it was a glossy stream tumbling down almost to her waist.

She'd grown it when she was young and all these years it would have been so much easier to cut it short. Why hadn't she cut it? Because of the look in Jonathan's eyes when he touched her hair? Because of the memories?

If she went out to join him with her hair loose down her back. . .

Oh, God! It was only hair! Only protein and colouring.

She would put her copy of the contract in her handbag. Just in case Jonathan needed reminding that until she issued a plain invitation — until. . .

She didn't have a lot of sense where Jonathan Halley was concerned. She'd always been susceptible. She'd better remember that. Remember that she'd loved him once before, that whatever he'd felt for her had melted into nothing then.

He wasn't willing to talk about yesterday. Nothing to say about the past. Nothing to say about the fact that she'd cried out to him and she'd been desperate. That he'd heard her and he'd still walked back into that damned house and Alicia had been watching through the window and——

It was a nightmare that didn't bear repeating.

The music in the dining-room was slower tonight. . . the rhythm deeper. There was a different singer, a young man with a deep voice who sang Spanish songs. She couldn't understand them, but she didn't need to hear the word *amor* to know that they were love songs.

There were more people tonight, perhaps because it was a Saturday. It was a quiet crowd, atmosphere and music for slow dining and dancing. They ordered lobster. Cynthia tried to focus on the taste but the music and Jonathan's silence caught her between reality and dreams. They ate slowly, no words. Only an electric pulse that kept time with the singer, a heavy beat as if the world were holding its breath.

Crazy to sip the potent liquor when there was already madness playing with the caution in her veins. Dangerous to let her eyes seek Jonathan's as he leaned back to let the waiter whisk his dinner-plate away.

Jonathan held her gaze as he lifted his own glass. She watched as he slowly drained it. When he put it down, she swallowed. She could feel his invitation before it came.

'Dance, moon lady?'

Saying yes might mean far more than she was ready to commit.

She pushed her chair back.

He reached for her hand.

She was in his arms before they reached the dance-floor.

He was silent, and she could not have talked if her life depended on it. She thought he would take her close against him and her nerves cried for the touch of flesh against flesh in the dance. But he held her carefully with empty space between them. She could feel his hand on the flesh of her back, the drifting cloud of her hair flowing over his touch as she moved with him in the dance.

She wanted to shelter against him, to hide her face in his shoulder. But her gaze was locked on his face and their eyes talked without her will as the beat led them into rhythm together. There was a blur of colour beyond Jonathan. She told herself to focus on it, to stare at the other dancers, at anything but *him*.

Her eyes wouldn't obey.

His arm around her and her hand on his shoulder. Their bodies hardly touched except for the necessary embrace of the dance. But her fingers went restlessly seeking the shape of his shoulder while her other hand felt alive in his loose grasp. She knew it was insane to deepen their embrace but she saw her own hand leave his and move to his shoulder. She was facing him directly now and her hands reached up to his shoulders and both his hands went to her waist. The pressure of his thumbs just above her waist encouraged a throbbing ache in her pulse. Only a heartbeat between staring and touching and the single motion that would bring their bodies together all along their length.

Between one sultry Spanish song and the next her body was brushing against his. His leg slipped between hers as he turned her in the dance. Her lips found his throat and touched a pulse there.

His hands went hard against her waist. She felt her body sway free with the rhythm so that his touch shifted on her. Her tension blossomed as the fabric over her breasts brushed against the white of his silk shirt.

'Let's get the hell out of here,' he growled. She felt the low vibration of his voice right through her body. His lips against her hair.

His hand at her back as she walked to the table. He picked up her handbag and she took it, clutched it against her side and thought of the papers it held. The contract. He spoke to the waiter and then his arm was around her shoulders, sheltering her, leading her away from the music. Outside.

Silence and the darkness that preceded a late moon. Sand underfoot, his arm steadying her. She'd worn high-heeled sandals, and if she stopped to take them off she thought she might stumble and fall. She'd had only one drink of tequila but she was dizzy with his scent. She'd hate Jonathan to think she was drunk, because his hand was rock-steady on her back, but the tremors were tearing through her.

The patio.

The door to their sitting-room. He opened it and she went in. Then a low light from one of the lamps and she stared at the luxurious furniture in front of her. Stared at the door open on to the room where he'd slept these last four nights. Stared at the other door, the closed door. Through it was the big master bedroom where she wouldn't invite him unless she was insane and bent on self-destruction.

His hands on her shoulders. Awareness of his body against her back as he swept the length of her hair aside and his lips pressed against her neck. She shivered and heard a husky sound like a laugh from him.

'I'm going to kiss you, moon lady.'

She turned, her mouth lifted and parted, her eyes locked on his.

He bent his head and she knew that when his lips touched she would be lost. She gasped and backed away. He came after her and she cried a broken sound of protest because he would touch and she would drown in him. If it began there would be no end.

He stopped as if she had frozen him.

Her eyes flew to the closed door of the room where she slept.

'Cynthia. . .' His voice was thick and husky. 'Don't run away.'

She curled her fingers and felt their pressure against her outer thighs. She could feel the trembling right through her body. He was watching her with brows lowered, his eyes unblinking. 'Don't run', he'd said. But he would kiss her. If he kissed her. . .

Slowly, she took the two steps back into his reach. Then she stopped, staring at his chin, biting her lip and knowing she was an inch away from coming apart. He stepped closer and she felt the air move with his breathing.

'Jonathan——'

His hands slid into her hair. He tilted her face up to his. She stared wide-eyed as he slowly lowered his mouth to hers. He stroked her lips with his, tasted her mouth.

'Open your mouth,' he commanded.

Her lips parted and the air drained out as he covered her mouth with his. Slowly. His lips brushing hers, his tongue teasing the fullness of her lips. Then inside, and his tongue touching the trembling inner surface of her mouth and his lips possessing hers then releasing with a sensuous tugging. His tongue tasting, circling and withdrawing so that her hunger grew ahead of his touch inside the darkness of her mouth.

She tried to keep her eyes open while his thumbs stroked her temples and his mouth played with hers in a slow, dark seduction. The world became his tongue in its slow stroking, his hands possessing her head and caressing her hair. She heard a sigh and it was hers, as he drank of her mouth and she melted against him.

Her breasts were pressed against his chest but it was not enough. His hands were too slow and her head moved restlessly, her mouth seeking possession of his hungrily and her arms tight around his shoulders, with fingers seeking the touch of warm flesh at his neck and threading into his hair and drawing him down into her; he groaned and her body strained hard, crushing her softness against him and rousing hunger too deep.

His touch slid down the length of her back and the sensation was fire. His hard need against her soft desire and her pulse rapid and crushed against him and needing more. . .restless. . .closer. . .breathing his name, a formless sound on her lips against his throat. . .his hands on her hips and she had no strength. . .needed his arms to take her. . .to possess her. . .take her with his strength. . .

She felt air against her flesh as his hands left her. He pulled back and she cried out. His lips left her mouth parted and swollen with aching desire and her flesh flushed and her nipples straining to touch, but he was gone and the emptiness was forever.

Jonathan. . .

His throat made a rough sound.

She gulped. He was a hand's reach away. Not touching. Watching her through narrowed eyes as if he could see the heavy pulse beating through her veins.

'Just so you understand,' he said. His voice was husky and unsteady. She could see his chest moving as if he was taking in gulps of air. If his eyes weren't in shadow she knew that they would show fire. She wanted to reach for him and couldn't.

'Just so you understand,' he said again. His voice was steadier now.

'What?' she whispered.

'Understand what you're running from. Just now— that wasn't just me. If it was, you'd have no need to run because I'm not forcing you into anything.'

She had no words.

He turned and walked away.

She sagged down on to the sofa. She closed her eyes and she could hear the sound of the ocean outside on the sand. Could smell the echo of Jonathan's aftershave. . .could feel the touch of his hands in her hair. . .his mouth on hers. . .his hands on her hips and her pulse deep and hungry, the joyful surge of welcome as he pulled her against his hard tension.

She shuddered and stumbled to her feet, and he was gone. She had a vague awareness of doors closing and his feet making sounds of moving. He could have taken her. If he'd left his touch on her the madness would never have let her free until she belonged completely to him.

She opened the door to her bedroom, went in, and closed it behind her. She should have felt safe then because if he had been prepared to release her after that kiss there was no danger he would invade her closed doors.

She'd always belonged to him. From that night at Lacey Wilkins's party when he had crossed through the people between them and reached for her hand. He'd led her out of the crowd and she'd have followed anywhere. The next day one of the boys from the party had stopped her on the street when she was in town buying a new lipstick. He'd asked her out once before, but now he said ruefully, 'You could have said you were Jonathan's girl. I know when I've lost.'

She had felt her face flush with heat because Jonathan had kissed her until she was dizzy and she'd promised to meet him that evening. She was going to have to make up some story for her absence from home or the witch would scent disobedience. She knew it was dangerous but nothing could have stopped her.

Stay away from that Halley kid. He's not your sort.

Six days of magic.

When she'd met him that evening he'd taken her walking on a remote beach. They'd talked and gathered driftwood for a fire where they'd roasted wieners.

'I've never roasted wieners before,' she said and he was astounded. Her world had been too much formality and he set out to teach her to be spontaneous, to laugh and talk and share dreams.

'I want my own home,' she confided. 'My place with my rules. My husband and my children.' Her face flamed and she stared at the sandy frankfurter she had just dropped in the sand.

'I'll wash it,' he offered. He took it out and rinsed off the sand in sea water. Then they roasted it again. He told her his dreams while they sat together staring at the fire after the food was gone.

'I'll build you a home,' he said, and it was crazy and too soon, but she believed him. She belonged to him and he was hers. She felt a certainty beyond the need for words.

The night before, Allan had come after them on the beach when the party had faded into the small hours of the morning. She couldn't believe it when her brother had said it was four in the morning. She'd just walked the night away on the beach with Jonathan, talking and secure in the shelter of his arm. Sometimes wild and breathless because he would stop and the talking would drain away and her mouth would seek his. Then, when Allan had come, she'd felt the awareness of herself and Jonathan as one unit, closed into a forever circle that left everyone else outside.

Allan had reached for her bag when he found them on the beach. 'It's time we got out of here,' he said. 'Lacey's parents are due back in the morning. Give me the keys — I'll drive.'

Jonathan had blocked Allan's grasp on her purse with one hard arm. 'There's no way she's driving anywhere with you at the wheel. You can go as a passenger or you can walk.' Jonathan was looking after her because something had happened there on the beach and they'd both changed. Then he'd taken Cynthia's shoulders in his hands and she'd seen by moonlight that he was frowning.

'Tomorrow?' he'd asked.

'Yes.'

'I'm working until four. I'll pick you up at five?'

'I'll meet you,' she'd said. A smile had curved her lips and she'd whispered, 'By the apple tree?'

Afterwards Allan had demanded to know what was the deal about the apple tree. She wouldn't tell because it was a secret between her and Jonathan that once she'd been thrown by a horse, and he'd picked her up and they'd talked until she'd heard her father's car and warned him away.

The rational part of her had known it couldn't last. She had only a few days' freedom to be with Jonathan.

'You're crazy,' Allan had warned her that first night as they drove towards Debby's house where Cynthia would drop off Allan and slip into her friend's house. 'You're going to get into trouble. The old man hates him.'

She'd stared at the highway and had known that nothing would stop her meeting Jonathan the next day. Her father would never approve. He approved only of young men who came from money and power, men who would make a good alliance when she was older. She'd shivered, knowing she would have to fight for Jonathan and she would have to fight very carefully. Secretly.

On Sunday, he'd taken her down to the Connars where they were haying. She'd sat on the wagon while he'd worked in the fields and she hadn't been sure if he was working for pay or for friendship, because Mr Connars had laughed and joked with Jonathan almost as if they were father and son.

Afterwards, when the hay was all in the barn, Jonathan had looked down from the loft and she'd looked up and seen laughter in his eyes, and something else that had made her heart stop. Mr Connars had gone up to the farmhouse and Jonathan had been the only person in the world. Jonathan standing in the loft, stripped to the waist.

His gaze had flickered over her cotton blouse and

the matching flared skirt. 'Think you could climb up here?'

Her eyes had followed the ladder up to his feet. He was wearing leather boots. Jeans. A black belt and nothing above but dark, sun-kissed skin.

'What will happen if I do?' she asked.

'I'll take your hair down.'

She was wearing it tied back with a cotton scarf. It wouldn't take much to release it. She remembered the beach and the campfire. Her hands were trembling and she wondered if they would hold as she climbed up to him.

When she was almost there he reached down and pulled her up into his arms. Then his lips found hers, hard and hungry. She could smell the tang of his strength, could taste hunger. She kissed him back as if it would be the last time, her hands intimate on the warm, naked flesh of his back.

His shoulders. His back. The rough tumble of dark hair on his chest.

The late afternoon sun beat in through the open door of the hayloft. Soft hay all around and the smell of the open fields here in the secret loft. Jonathan's mouth on hers and she twisted against him when he stroked her body. When he groaned she felt excitement and power rush through her veins because he was as intoxicated as she was. She'd dreamed him, and, with his eyes on her and his mouth drawing away from their kiss to find the long, trembling vulnerability of her throat, she knew that he'd dreamed her too.

Her hair was free. Then her blouse, and his hands hard and hungry on her back and her midriff. He freed her breasts of the bra. She gasped and moaned as his hands took the place of the lace and she sagged against him.

'Yes,' he groaned, and they were down in the hay. It

scratched against her skin. She welcomed it because it was Jonathan touching her, and she could smell the hay all around like a lover's scent.

His hand slid on her thigh and as she closed her eyes the world stopped. His face in her hair and his voice telling her he loved her hair and the soft wonder of her. His mouth on her breast and the world dived down, until his hand slid along the softness of her inner thigh and found the silky covering of her panties, and the universe shattered.

She needed desperately to know what he wanted of her. Should she be silent? Should she move to his touch the way her pulse urged? Or draw back, because what would he think of her if she just moved in his arms and let him know that she had no way to deny his desires?

He stroked her through the flimsy barrier of her panties and she gasped, and then his mouth was loving her breasts and his hands cradling her hips and she was tangled with him and time tilted into Jonathan's touch and his taste and the wild pulse of the afternoon sun slanting in on them.

The rough sensation of hair on his legs and she gasped as he slid his leg between hers. She opened her eyes and in his she saw something that echoed in some primitive part of her woman's heart. Then her skirt was gone and his jeans, and it was all sensation and heavy, hot insanity and in a heartbeat she would know what it was like when a woman's lover possessed her.

Silence. Heartbeats without breath. His breathing was unsteady, his hand intimate on the bare flesh of her thigh. Her pulse echoed his.

Then it stopped.

'You haven't done this before, have you, moon lady?'

'No.' She shivered and wished she were everything he wanted. 'I'm sorry.'

He shook his head and she saw him stare down at his own hand on her flesh. She thought she should cover herself, but she felt no sense of embarrassment with Jonathan's eyes on her, although she could see her own legs tangled with his and the sight had a sensuous abandon that made her gasp.

'Jonathan?' she whispered. 'Is it OK?'

He breathed in sharply. 'Yeah,' he said. His hands brushed threads of hair back from her face. 'I didn't realise, that's all. The way you responded to me, I thought——'

'I never did that before,' she whispered. She felt her face heating. His fingers touched where the colour must be staining her cheekbones. She swallowed and admitted, 'I've only—— Just kissing and not like. . . never like it is with you.'

His hand stilled on her face. She lifted her mouth to his lips. The kiss was slow and soft and so gentle, it hurt deep inside her. Then it ended and he drew back. His eyes had changed and she knew she was going to lose him.

Her father was returning tomorrow and seeing Jonathan would be impossible.

'Jonathan,' she whispered. 'It's all right. . .you can. . .it's all right.'

'No. . .no, Cynthia.'

He twisted and she saw his muscles tighten as he reached for her blouse. He handed it to her and then he turned away and pulled on his shirt. She sat up and found her bra lying tumbled in the straw. She put it on, then pushed her arms into her blouse and fastened the buttons and they were all wrong. She felt sick inside. He was fully dressed now, even wearing the shirt he'd taken off earlier in the day. She felt the echo of that warm, hard sensation of his body naked against hers, and it was pain and loss because it was only memory now.

'Jonathan, ha—I—have you made love to a lot of girls?'

A muscle jerked along his cheekbone. He reached his hand down and pulled her to her feet. 'None like you,' he said.

'I'm sorry,' she whispered again.

'There's nothing to be sorry for.' He smiled and his expression was wry as if he was laughing at himself. 'We'll do it differently, moon lady. That's all.'

She swallowed and bit her lip. 'I might not be able to see you for a few days. My dad's coming back tomorrow.'

He frowned.

'Just a few days,' she begged. 'I just—once he's gone again—he'll be off on a business trip in a few days.'

He ran his hand through his hair, and she saw it curl around his fingers. 'You're telling me that if we're going to see each other it's behind his back?'

She gulped and nodded, and she could see that he didn't like it.

'I have to go,' she said. She couldn't lose him. Couldn't walk away now and have it be forever. 'Please,' she begged. 'I—Jonathan, when he's gone again I'll. . .we can. . .'

He touched her cheek and then kissed her and it was a hard kiss. She felt anger and need, and when she pulled back there was confusion and a feeling inside like tearing because she couldn't let him go out of her life but she was terrified of battle against her father's immobile rules.

'We'll work it out,' he said.

'Yes,' she agreed, but she wasn't sure she believed in a magic that could conquer her father.

Her father's Mercedes was there in the drive when she got home. She parked her car behind it. He was back early, home too soon. She'd meant to be home when he arrived, not out disobeying him.

She went into the house slowly. The door of his study was closed, but she could feel his presence behind it. Mrs Corveson came into the entrance hallway.

'He wants to see you, Cynthia.' The housekeeper jerked her head towards the study door. 'As soon as you're in, he said. He called Debby Fondyke's but you weren't there.'

Cynthia fought a wave of nausea. She should have known she couldn't get away with it. She looked down at her clothes. She'd brushed off all the hay. There was no sign she could see of how she'd spent her afternoon. She went towards the door and she opened it and closed it behind her. He knew she hadn't been at Debby's. She was swallowing repeatedly, trying to think of something to say, a story to make up, but there was nothing.

He was working at the desk. When he looked up his eyes were hard with fury. Before her mother's death two years ago he had been different, dogmatic and stubborn and strict, but not always angry. As if her mother had softened a hard man. As if her death brought the hardness flooding back.

'I know who you've been with.' His voice was tight with boiling anger. 'I warned you to keep away from Art Halley's kid.'

She should have begged Jonathan to make love to her today. She could see what was in her father's harsh expression. She would never see Jonathan again.

She was confined to the grounds the next day. Grounded until her father returned to Toronto and took her with him. She was going to school in Toronto when September came.

She would never see Jonathan again. Never.

Her horse had always been her escape from the restrictions of her life, but today she walked instead, down the hill and over the grass that led through the trees. Walking slowly, carefully. Allan might sneak over walls and into cars he'd been forbidden to, but Cynthia hadn't her brother's daredevil rashness.

She walked unevenly down the hill to the bench where she'd had her first real talk with Jonathan Halley two years before. She sat carefully on it and she didn't cry. She'd cried last night.

She wanted to call Jonathan. To see him at least for goodbye.

She knew she dared not. She might be able to phone him from Debby's before she left, but she wasn't counting on that freedom. Not after the session with her father last night.

She would write to Jonathan. A goodbye letter.

She heard branches moving. Then her name on the air, and when she looked up he was there. Jonathan. Her eyes flickered towards the house but they were alone.

'Jonathan,' she whispered. She tried to make her lips curve into a smile.

He sat on the bench beside her. 'What's wrong?' he demanded.

She clenched her hands. 'I can't see you again.'

He touched her shoulder and she cried out before she could stop the reflex. 'Go,' she whispered desperately. 'If my father catches you here he'll kill you.'

'What happened to your shoulder?'

Her fingers fluttered to the place where he'd touched. 'N-nothing.'

'Don't lie to me.'

She gulped when he reached for her.

Slowly he unbuttoned the loose blouse she wore. She

stared at his face, not down at her own body. When he pushed the blouse off her shoulder, her first thought was that she wasn't wearing a bra. But on his face she saw the stillness darken to fury.

'Who hurt you?'

'Let go,' she whispered. 'Let me go.'

His hands fell away from her.

She fastened her buttons with shaking hands, hiding the bruises. 'I shouldn't have gone out with you,' she said in a low voice. 'He told me not to see you. I shouldn't have disobeyed.'

He moved sharply to his feet. She shivered when she saw the look on his face. 'Your father did that?' His voice was a growl. 'The bastard hurt you because of me?'

'I didn't — He warned me not to have anything to do with you.'

His face was pale under the tan, his mouth a rigid slash of tension. 'It's not the first time, is it? That's why you're so frightened of him? He's hurt you—this has happened before?'

She tangled her hands together. 'Since my mother died two years ago. But only if—not if I do what I'm told.' She closed her eyes and admitted what she'd known when the first blow struck. 'I shouldn't have seen you. But I wanted. . .I wanted so much to be with you.'

She heard him curse. Then the sound of his footsteps heavy on the grass. She opened her eyes and he was prowling towards the big apple tree he'd once taken fruit from. He leaned one arm against it and he was motionless for long seconds. Then he turned back to face her. She saw decision on his face.

'Come away with me.'

Her heart slammed against her chest. 'Your job,' she said. 'Your university year?'

'Forget that. Just come with me.'

A dream. Impossible. 'He wouldn't let me.'

Jonathan shook his head. 'Come over the fence with me right now. We'll be gone before he knows.'

'I'm under age,' she said. She knew the power of her father's money. 'He'd find me. There would be police and lawyers. And he'd make sure you—I—when I'm nineteen——' She flushed. His eyes were locked on hers with angry intensity and she breathed, 'I'll be of age in a little over two years. When I'm nineteen I can do what I want. If you——' Her face heated as she wished she didn't sound as if she was begging. 'I'll go away with you then.'

'And until then?' His eyes flickered to her shoulders. 'Do you think I'm going to let you be beaten again?'

'I won't do anything to make him angry.' She smiled bitterly and said, 'I'm quite good at being well-behaved, you know. It's just that I. . .that I wanted—I wanted to be with you.'

He looked up at the house.

She understood then that he wasn't going to simply walk away. She whispered, 'No, Jonathan! Don't,' but he was walking up the hill fast and he didn't hear her.

She was afraid to follow him. She knew she had no choice but she went slowly up the hill. Very slowly.

She was almost out of the trees when she heard the shouting. She stopped under an old oak tree and stared at Jonathan on the front stairs, his voice a low growl she couldn't understand. Her father was in the doorway. She knew that angry stance. It was a wild scene frozen in time, with Allan below them both, standing beside her car on the drive and his hand moving as if he held keys. Allan was watching while Jonathan and her father faced each other with rage written in every line of their bodies.

Her father moved one step towards Jonathan.

'Jonathan,' she whispered. As if her fear could protect him.

Allan turned towards the car.

Her father started towards Jonathan and she could hear his voice rising.

Later, Cynthia knew that it was the most cowardly thing she had ever done, but she turned and ran as if they were both after her and her life depended on her speed. She ran through the trees and down the hill and kept going until she was in the apple orchard near the western boundary of the estate. She stopped there and sank to the grass. She was trembling, breathing with noisy, tearing sobs as if the blows were falling on her with each breath.

She didn't now how long she waited. Minutes. They felt like hours. Timeless, until she heard the explosion. Then she jerked around and she saw the smoke in the sky from the direction of the highway.

A car. It had to be a car or a truck. Smoke, and she saw red in the sky. A car exploding. Maybe something bigger. Perhaps a tanker truck. She stood, and began to run.

She ran towards the house, but it was all uphill and she had to slow, to walk, breathing hard and saying over and over again it wasn't anyone she knew. Nothing to do with her, with Jonathan or Allan or her father. An explosion. A fuel truck driving the island highway. No one she knew.

It seemed forever before she got to the house. She found Mrs Corveson in the drive, staring towards the gates. Cynthia had to call out twice before the house-keeper heard.

'An accident,' she said. Her gaze was pulled back towards the gates. 'Your father's been to call the ambulance and gone back.'

Cynthia's car was gone. The driveway was empty.

'Allan?' she asked on a whisper. Allan in the night-mare accident that she'd dreaded for years. Her father gone to try to help.

'And that Halley boy,' muttered the housekeeper. 'They drove into a tree down at the highway.'

CHAPTER SEVEN

HER father came home very late. The darkness outside had begun to lighten with the dawn. Cynthia had called the hospital and been told that neither Jonathan nor Allan had been admitted. She'd seen the explosion flaring high in the sky. If they weren't in hospital, she thought it must mean that doctors and hospitals could do nothing.

She waited terrified through the night, with Mrs Corveson hovering near by. Waiting for the news that would let the tears loose. She should have gone with Jonathan when he asked. If she had, that confrontation on the stairs wouldn't have taken place. Allan, with the keys, would have gone to the car and simply driven away. Her father wouldn't have been outside to see and her brother would have driven calmly, not with his father's rage following him.

And Jonathan would be alive.

When her father came in, his face was closed and tight.

'Jonathan?' she asked. 'Allan? Are they——? I called the hospital and they aren't there. What. . .what happened?'

His face went grimmer and he said, 'They were taken to the Nanaimo hospital. Allan's just come out of surgery. Your bloody fool of a brother will have a good limp to show for his nonsense.'

She gulped and hugged herself hard. 'Jonathan?'

'He walked away.' His jaw jerked, and he added bitterly, 'Whatever suffering Allan does now will be young Halley's fault. He was driving. His fault, but he

117

walked away. They took him into the hospital and they let him go.' He glared at her and growled, 'And I hope he keeps walking. I hope he goes one hell of a long way. But it doesn't matter because *you're* leaving. I'm sending you to Switzerland.'

Jonathan was alive! They were both alive.

'Switzerland?' she asked, but she could only see Jonathan in her mind. Jonathan alive when she'd spent the night thinking him dead. Her mind tried to get around the mechanics of the accident. It had been her car that smashed. Her car, and she had thought Allan had taken it without permission. Jonathan and Allan in her car and she had seen Allan with keys in his hand. Her father and Jonathan arguing on the front porch. Then she'd run, and Allan must have given the keys to Jonathan and asked him to drive. She couldn't make sense of that.

'You leave tomorrow,' her father said. He glanced at his watch and said, 'Today. The night's almost gone. The helicopter will be here at noon to fly you to Vancouver International.'

It didn't matter. Nothing mattered. Jonathan was alive and the years would pass and one day she would come and find him again.

'Where is he?' she asked, not caring that the question would anger her father.

'How the hell would I know? Mrs Corveson is going with you as far as Geneva.'

When had he arranged this? Yesterday he'd said she was going to Toronto. Now he was sending her to Europe. She dropped her arms and stood very straight. 'You're sending me to Switzerland to get me away from Jonathan? You don't think Toronto is far enough?'

He gave a bark of angry laughter. 'Nowhere is far enough.'

Jonathan was alive. She gulped and announced, 'I'm saying goodbye to him. I'll go but—not until I see Jonathan. And I want to see Allan, too.'

He stared back at her and there was something complex in his face. It was as though he stared right through her.

'I'll drive you,' he said.

He took her to the small ranch-style house where Jonathan lived with his father and his older sister. He stopped the Mercedes outside the gate and Cynthia said, 'I'm seeing him alone. You're not coming in.'

She couldn't believe she had the nerve to talk like that to her father but somehow it didn't matter now. She got out of the car and he let her. She was halfway along the path to Jonathan's front porch when she looked back and saw him watching. She shivered and continued on up the path.

She hammered on the door a long time before it opened and Jonathan's sister came out. Cynthia recognised Alicia although she'd hardly spoken to her before. She'd been working in the Parkland bank for several years and sometimes she took Cynthia's deposits when she took her monthly allowance into the bank. Sometimes Alicia smiled at Cynthia, but never with much friendliness.

'What do you want?' asked Alicia. She wasn't smiling today.

'I want to see Jonathan.'

Alicia looked from Cynthia to the car. Her face went hard, but after a moment she shrugged. 'I'll get him, then.'

Cynthia had hoped to be invited in, had wanted to say goodbye to Jonathan out of her father's sight. She stepped towards the door, but she stopped when Alicia threw her a warning look.

'Wait out here,' the older woman commanded.

Jonathan came a few minutes later. His hair was wet as if he'd been in the shower. She could see the damp black ends curling and a bead of water at the side of his neck where he had missed with the towel. He was wearing clean jeans and a checkered cotton shirt and he had a darkening bruise on one side of his face.

'Jonathan. . .' She swallowed and wanted him to say something, but he was silent.

He looked from her to her father's car and his face was carved from granite. Finally, he asked, 'What do you want, Cynthia?'

She clenched her fingers. 'Mrs Corveson said you and Allan—I saw the smoke from the explosion and—— Oh, God, Jonathan! How did you ever survive the crash?'

His jaw flexed. He said tonelessly, 'The fire was after. We got out of the car before that happened.'

'Did you. . .?' He was staring at her and she lost track of her words. 'I'm going away,' she said. 'I'm going to—I'm going to school in Switzerland.'

He inclined his head.

'Will you wait for me?' she asked on a whisper.

A curtain flickered in the window behind Jonathan. Alicia observing from inside. Her father from outside.

'No,' Jonathan said.

Her eyes widened.

'I'm not waiting for you and you're not coming back to me.' He rammed one hand into the back pocket of his jeans. 'Whatever happened between us is over. Forget it.'

'You don't mean it?' She gulped and the tears filled her eyes. 'You—we——' She bit her lip painfully. 'I love you. I thought. . .I thought you loved me. I *know* you do. When you—when we——'

'You know nothing,' he said. His face grew harder. 'It's over.'

'Is it——?' She twisted her head to look back at her father, a threatening shadow inside his Mercedes. 'My father said you were driving. That it was your fault. But—but I *know* it was an accident!'

Jonathan was a skilful driver. He'd driven in stock-car races and he had twice driven her car and handled it with a casual skill that made her feel inept at the wheel. She couldn't imagine him running a car into a tree.

'It wasn't your fault,' she said with faith and no knowledge. His face was shuttered and she remembered her father's words, and doubt crept into her heart.

She heard a car door slam. Then the sound of the gate. Jonathan looked from her to the man coming towards her and he said, 'Go now. There's nothing between us.'

'She's leaving today,' her father's voice said. 'Flying to Switzerland.'

She couldn't understand the tone of his voice. She'd expected him to be threatening towards Jonathan, but there was no threat, only something else she couldn't understand. Her father glanced down at her and said with no expression at all, 'She's going to school in Switzerland.'

'Good,' Jonathan said, and the love in her heart finally began to turn to ashes. He turned away and crossed the porch towards his front door. She saw his hand reach out and turn the knob.

When he went through that door she would never see him again.

'Jonathan!' she cried out. 'Jonathan! Please!'

A muscle jerked in his back, but he didn't turn.

'I love you,' she whispered.

He turned his head and his eyes were empty. The laughter and the loving and the caring were gone, as if they had never been. Even his voice had no trace of loving in it.

'Get out of here,' he said. 'Go to Switzerland.'

Cynthia got up from the bed and walked to the window that opened on to the ocean and the beach. Cabo San Lucas. Jonathan was back in her life after years of seeing his picture in print, seeing his face across a room full of people.

Married to Jonathan. Once, that had been her dream.

Once, when she believed in the love he'd never declared.

'Get out of here,' he'd said. 'Go to Switzerland.'

Nothing could ever change that. She'd cried out her love and he'd told her to get out of his life. She opened the window and tried to clear the past with deep breaths of warm sea air.

The moon must be rising. She could see moonlight on the water but when she turned her head there was no moon to see in the sky.

Jonathan had said that there was nothing to talk about in their past. If she let herself love him again it would always be there—knowledge that he'd rejected her once. That she'd begged him and he'd said, 'Get out!'

It could happen again. It had to be all physical for him, not a merging of souls. Otherwise how could he have wanted her and then not wanted her, as if his desire had an 'off' switch attached? On and off and on again.

He'd never said he loved her. Not then. Not now.

She saw something cut through the moonlight. A swimmer's arm. Jonathan's arm. The past fought with the present in her heart and she couldn't tell if they were one and the same. . .was it possible for today to be a new life that could be detached from yesterday?

He was swimming hard. He disappeared in the trough of a wave and when she caught sight of him again he had turned and was swimming back towards her. She felt the urge to run, to hide in the safety of the big bedroom with the glass patio doors closed and her own needs buried.

She wanted him to come to her. Wanted him to open doors and shed light into her shadows. God help her if she was waiting for him to say he loved her. God help her if she needed to understand the past, because he said there was nothing in the past for them.

She remembered Eric's deliberate courting of her in Switzerland when she was twenty, remembered fighting the memories of Jonathan, forcing them down with an act of will. *I will love Eric.* That was what she'd told herself. She had tried to believe then that Jonathan was a dream, an aberration of teenage hormones in her bloodstream. Eric was all there was.

Her heart had known the truth. That was why she'd felt so panicked as she'd gone up the aisle of the church towards Eric. She should have turned then and run. Instead, she'd stayed to learn that her marriage was founded on a sham; that Eric was part of a business deal and her pale pretence of love as insubstantial as the mist.

Stupid to marry Eric when her heart knew that she hadn't forgotten the pain of Jonathan. Stupid to marry Jonathan when she knew she could never love him again without the fear of betrayal. But she'd done it. She'd made the mistake with her eyes wide open, married him knowing he would ask for more than she could safely give.

Jonathan hadn't pretended it would remain a marriage of convenience even at the beginning. She won-

dered if he played for deals in money and land this way
and how much she mattered compared to that conference centre he'd built in the Maritime provinces last
year.

She watched Jonathan turn again and swim out to
sea. He would come back when he was tired, when he
had spent the breathless passion he'd turned on her so
briefly earlier. He'd made her show him her need, then
he'd left her with the aching pulse of inevitability.

When he returned he would go to that other bedroom and she would be safely alone for another night.
One more night lying to herself, pretending that she
didn't breathe and eat and sleep with the awareness of
Jonathan against her heart. That she hadn't ached for
the loss of his magic all these years. That this last week
hadn't taught her new needs. New magic. That she
didn't yearn for the life she could glimpse in the spaces
between her fears and his unwillingness to look at their
past.

Jonathan had said that all they had was the future.
He made it sound so easy, so rational to let the past
go.

She could run. She'd be safe then. And alone.

He had torn up his right to enforce that agreement,
he told her in destroying the document that he would
not use his power against her. Would not stop her if
she chose to betray her own promise. But he wouldn't
give up. She could cheat on him by running away from
her promise, but he would still be in her life. At
dinners and charity balls.

Could she handle that? She'd lived the public role of
Eric's wife for years with nothing under the shell. It
hadn't been all that difficult. Nothing there when she
looked at him. Playing a part.

Sitting across a dinner-table from Jonathan would be
completely different. She wouldn't be able to look

away. She would stare and he would meet her eyes and her heart would pound with the image of him getting up from the table and holding out his hand to her and saying, 'Come away with me,' as he had once.

She had refused him then.

Was that when he had stopped caring? Was that why? Because she refused to go with him? She'd been afraid and too young and she'd seen a future of disaster piling up. Jonathan giving up his education for her. Her father sending police because she was under age, and heaven knew what influence his power could amass against Jonathan.

But now Jonathan was the powerful one. Her father was dead.

Jonathan would never use his power against her. He didn't have to because she would always be haunted by him. She closed her eyes and wondered if there was a place in the world where she could be free of her own heart.

She turned back into her room.

She opened a drawer and took out a short satin nightgown with thin straps. She put it on and stared at herself in the mirror. If she went to him dressed like this he would have no doubt that it was an invitation.

What if he looked at her the way he had back on the porch of his family's Parkland house fourteen years ago? She'd cried out her love then and he'd thrown it back at her. And now. . .

God help her but she loved him again and if she let it free the words might spill out all over again—and again he could deny her by all the things he wouldn't say.

I love you, moon lady. Only you and always you.

That was the fantasy. The dream.

She put a matching lacy négligé over the gown. Better, she thought. Less skin and he couldn't see every curve if his eyes probed. She tied the négligé at the front and went back to the open window. She couldn't see him on the water. He must have swum towards the shore where the moonlight hadn't penetrated yet.

She heard his feet on the sand before she saw him. Then her eyes found the movement of shadow on shadow and she was torn between fear and a wild need to go running down to him, flying into danger and confusion.

She saw him in silhouette from the single light burning in the sitting-room. He was barefoot, wearing only brief bathing-trunks with a towel slung across his shoulders. He rubbed at his wet hair with the towel as his bare feet caught on the tile of the patio.

Her breath dried up in her throat. He was going into his bedroom.

'Jonathan,' she said, her voice too quiet.

He stopped with one hand on the patio door to his bedroom. Waiting. Not watching her but waiting out her words before he left.

She swallowed. 'You were gone a long time.'

'Yes,' he agreed. She heard the sound of the door-latch opening. 'Goodnight, Cynthia.'

She pressed her lips painfully together and didn't know the words or how to say them. In the end she whispered, 'Please. . .Jonathan. . .' and the sound carried only because the night was so still.

She saw the shape of his shoulders shift as if he had taken a large breath. She'd begged him once before and he'd said cold words and gone through a door away from her. Now he had the door open and she felt a panicked certainty that if he went through it there would be other doors closed between them forever.

'Can we talk?' she pleaded. 'Please?' Her pulse was pounding and she realised that if he turned and demanded words from her there would be nothing more sensible than confused blabbering. If she had to talk she could only blurt words, and she might say anything because she knew only that if she let him go into that room she would regret it.

'No,' he said. His voice was empty of feeling, as if he had left the emotions out there in the water. 'No,' he repeated. 'We can't talk. Not tonight.'

She reached one hand towards him and saw his head turn. She whispered his name. His silhouette moved impatiently.

'Moon lady, you don't want to talk to me tonight.'

'Why not?' she whispered. Any words to stop him leaving.

'This waiting game sounded reasonable enough when I planned it.' His voice grew in harshness as the words came out. 'But not tonight. Tonight I've no patience and you're dreaming if you expect understanding from me.'

'I don't care,' she whispered.

She saw his hand drop from the door. 'Cynthia — you're not safe with me tonight.' His arm gestured abruptly. 'Turn around and get back into that room and close the door tightly behind you because if you leave a crack I'll come through it. I'm not playing tonight. No talking. No games.'

She tried to breathe but her lungs were too small. She wanted to reach, to say a word, to bring him close. Her heartbeat drowned out everything but his voice.

'I told you I'd wait until you issued the invitation. But tonight you could push me with a feather and send me over the edge.'

She was straining against darkness with her eyes, stretching her ears to catch emotion and undertones between his words.

'What if I push?' she asked. 'What will happen?'

He gave a sound that might have been a bark of laughter. 'You'll get the lot,' he vowed. 'Whatever talent I have for seduction. Whatever I can do to make your body cry for me — I'll do it.' His words turned harsh. 'If you want that contract between us as your shield you'd better hide until daylight comes and pray it brings me sanity.'

She moved two steps closer to him. Then she stopped. 'You sent me away when I came to you that morning in Parkland. I told you I loved you and you sent me away. How can I forget that?'

'That's over,' he said. His voice was low. 'If you come to me now, no power on this earth could make me send you away.'

She took a deep breath and crossed the cool tiles towards him. Close enough that she could reach out and touch his silhouette and it would be warm, hard muscles. Her fingers curled with the knowledge that if she did reach she would find the naked reality of his chest.

Her voice was a thread of moonlight. 'If you won't. . .' She swallowed and whispered, 'If we can't talk. . .then can we make love?'

She could feel the sudden stillness. Then he pushed the door he'd been holding and it swung away and latched closed.

'Are you sure?'

She let out a ragged breath. 'I hope so.' She gulped and knew from his stillness that it wasn't enough. She bit her lip and there was nothing in the blackness of his shadow to help her. Nothing to reassure her and make the fears melt into the need she had fought through all the hours since she'd seen him again in that construction shack.

'I don't know how to ask,' she said quietly. 'I know

I have to say the words but I don't know——' He was
so close. A heartbeat away.

'Be sure, moon lady. I've spent years fighting the
vision of you in another man's arms. Once I make you
mine. . .I won't let you go.'

She shivered deeply. 'It wasn't true,' she said. 'My
marriage——' She swallowed. 'You were right.' He was
so silent. She was terrified with nothing but words to
fill the silence. 'I found out on my wedding-day. It was
a merger; Dad's money into Eric's newspaper. I didn't
know until—— I'd thought—I wanted to believe I
could forget you. That's why I married him. But we
didn't—whatever you saw in the society pages, that's
all there was between Eric and me.'

She reached out and her hand touched his chest. She
felt hard, naked skin. Heard his breathing, disturbed.

'Moon lady——' His body jerked. 'I used to see you
sometimes. With him. I looked at you and I told myself
you didn't look like a woman in love. Then I'd think it
was just because I wanted you to want only me. But
yesterday—when you told me you couldn't have children—I thought you'd tried, that you and Eric——'

She bit her lower lip. If he felt like that, why had he
sent her away when she was sixteen? She trembled and
pushed that old pain away. 'I was sick when I was
eighteen,' she told him unsteadily. 'They did tests
then.' She flattened both palms against him and
stepped closer. She could feel resistance in him. She
pressed her lips against his chest. 'You taste of salt,'
she said raggedly. 'I need you to make love to me. I'm
asking you. . .Jonathan.'

She felt the shudder go through him. His hands
found her in the shadows. He brought her close against
him and his lips came down and hers lifted to meet
them.

'I've waited so long,' he breathed.

'Yes,' she said and it was a growl against his mouth. His kiss was hungry on her and she answered his desire with her own heat.

His mouth left hers and lips travelled the journey towards her throat. She stretched her neck to give him the touch she needed. His hands were slow and shattering through the satin and lace of her gown. Then he slid his hands up to possess her breasts and she moaned deep into his mouth.

'Yes,' he said, and he swept her up into his arms and took her into her bedroom. Inside, he let her slide slowly to her feet along the hard length of his body before he pushed the négligé back over her shoulders. It slid down her arms and dropped to the floor. She was left standing in an insubstantial satin gown that hung suspended from thin straps.

'It's all right,' he said and she realised then that she was trembling. 'I promise you it'll be all right.'

He ran his hands down her arms. Her lips parted and in the faint light that found its way in through the open door she saw his eyes widen. He brushed her mouth with his, tasting her and moving away so that she whimpered and sought his kiss again.

Then he kissed her deeply and took away the world and time and all the universe except the man holding her in his arms and drinking from her mouth with his. She let his arms take her weight and when there was nothing holding her but Jonathan's strength she felt a wild flood of joy surging over her so that she moved against him and with him and heard him groan in response.

'Witch,' he growled. His hands closed on her hips and moved down over the curve of her buttocks. He lifted her breathlessly high and when the world stopped spinning she was sitting on the dressing-table with

Jonathan standing in front of her and her legs parted
to let him close.

She let her hands slide down the hard tension of his
upper arms. He took her face in his hands and kissed
her deeply and she felt her legs clutch at him to hold
him close while the world tilted. He slid one hand
down to her thigh and when his fingers stroked the
bare flesh she shuddered at the wave of weakness that
tore through her body. She turned her face into his
chest and her mouth was hungry on the salty skin there.

He stroked her thigh with heated softness. His mouth
found hers and she arched into him when his touch
found the moistness at her centre and his mouth drew
her gasp.

He threw his head back. She trembled at the molten
desire in his eyes as his gaze swept down over her. She
could feel the abandon of her own body, perched on
the dressing-table with his hands on her and her thighs
cradling him as he stood in front of her. She was aware
of the thin satin of her gown, and when she looked she
saw her breasts thrusting the hard erection of her
nipples through the slippery fabric.

'I'm not very experienced at this,' she breathed.

She saw his throat spasm, his eyes locked on the
edge of her gown high on her thigh.

'I could disappoint you,' she whispered. 'I
don't——'

'No,' he said. His hands made the slow journey from
her hips to the satin seduction of her breasts. Her body
moved against his touch, striking an overpowering
wave of sensation. 'There have been other women,' he
said solemnly, 'but there wasn't one I didn't wish was
you.'

She leaned into him. Her legs tangled around his
thighs, holding him close as his hand slid down to find
the silken softness of her thigh. She shuddered and

groaned into his mouth as he touched the heart of her
woman's pulse. He moved against her and his mouth
took hers deeply, his tongue drawing the sounds and
her hands gone wild on his back. . .his shoulders. . .
his chest and the hungry need of her mouth for his.

She cried out and he made a sound back to her and
there weren't even words, just sounds and her need,
his urge to conquer and hers to submit with a wild,
primitive power that consumed her.

She saw his throat clench as his voice came to her,
ragged and deep. 'From the day I heard you were free
again there hasn't been any other woman.'

'I might still disappoint you,' she said in a thick
whisper because the old fear was trembling along with
her desire. The fear that he would take her love and
close his heart to her.

His hands settled on her shoulders and slid the thin
straps of the satin down on to her arms. His thumbs
hooked the straps and the satin dragged over the erect
peaks of her nipples. He bent down and she saw his
lips part. Her breasts swelled with aching need and she
let out a long whimper of sensation as his mouth took
her nipple and drew it in, his tongue caressing as she
was taken deeper and her legs wrapped around to
possess him and her head thrown back and her body
wild and aching. . .pulsing against him with a motion
that she could not suppress. He moved against her in
response and the wildness was a force out of control;
his mouth slipped off her breast and the leaving was
more shattering than the possession.

'How?' he growled. He slid his hands under her hips
and stood erect. She was tangled around him as he
took her the two steps to the big bed and sank down
with her in a breathless seductive sensation of tangled
legs and arms. He cupped both her breasts with his
hands and bent down to kiss each peak with shattering

slowness. 'How could you disappoint me?' he asked
again and she heard his voice tremble. 'You tear me
apart with a heartbeat. How could you disappoint me?'

He slid the satin down further and she was molten in
his arms and her touch was on the salty tension of
his flesh. . .her mouth against the heartbeat in his
throat. . .his kiss stroking flames in her and when she
touched her lips to his she felt his pulse beat against
her mouth and she found the edge of his bathing-trunks
with restless touch and there was no beginning. . .no
end. . .only Jonathan breathing her name and his kiss
on her and her fingers and her mouth and the wild
motion of her body's need. . .stroking his passion to
flames that exploded as they touched her heart. . .

She dragged her eyes open. She heard his breathing
echoing hers and her mouth sought the touch of his
flesh and her body stirred against his, and as she moved
she felt his desire flare higher. He was tangled with
her, body and heart. She stretched against him and
with each breath felt the responding need in him. She
had loved him forever. Would need him forever with a
desperation that could not ease. Always.

'Beautiful,' he groaned against her flesh. His hands
shaped her body from her throat to the softness of her
thighs and he caressed her with his voice husky against
her. 'Warm,' he whispered against her throat. 'Soft,'
he breathed against her breast.

When she writhed against him for the hard response
that would take her beyond sanity he groaned, 'God, I
love feeling you needing me.'

Then his touch turned urgent and she felt the flames
crawl up inside her and her body molten in his arms.
She caressed him to find the touch that made him
groan, and whispered wildness when it was too much,
moaning and losing control of her head, rocking on the
bed and his hands and his mouth on her. She whispered

over and over in heat, 'Oh, Jonathan. . .please. . . please, I can't — oh, God, Jonathan!'

She felt his need to drive her beyond madness; higher than she could go, except that she rose up and there were more heights and she was there at the top with his body hard over hers in the instant before she became his forever.

'You're mine,' he said and the long stroke of possession sent her over the edge into madness. She was crying his name and running her hands wildly on his body and moving with his thrusting need to drive him further until there was nowhere but the edge of the cliff and the long slide down into his arms when the explosion had spent.

Eyes closed, and breathing Jonathan deep into her lungs as her heart calmed to sanity. His pulse against her cheek slowing. . .losing force until it transformed into normal heart strokes. The room filled with moonlight and when she opened her eyes she saw him watching. His gaze slid intimately over her body as it lay tangled with his.

'I've waited fourteen years for you,' he said softly.

She pushed away a rush of confusion. 'Was it worth it?'

He curved one hand along her cheek. Then he placed his lips on hers and slowly explored the secrets of her mouth.

'Yes,' he breathed. 'Worth every damned minute.'

His thumb brushed her lips and they parted for him. Then his mouth covered hers and he drew her very close while his hand slid into her hair and he kissed her as if there was a world of time for this exploration.

'It's not over yet,' he said.

She searched his eyes and they were lazy, glowing with a slower passion than the wild storm that had just possessed them. She gave him her lips and whispered, 'I might not survive.'

He chuckled, and she felt his laughter to the depths of her heart.

possessed them. She gave him her lips and whispered,
'I might not see—'

He laughed, and silenced his comment with the ardent
assault of his—

CHAPTER EIGHT

IT WAS chilly when Jonathan and Cynthia stepped
outside at Toronto's airport. When she shivered,
Jonathan put his arm around her as if he could stop the
weather from penetrating her light clothing. She smiled
up at him and he drew her even closer.

Three days in Jonathan's arms and she was beginning
to believe that her fears were needless. His arms and
his eyes, and with every moment her heart was relaxing
into trust. She loved him. Soon she would say the
words.

They took a limousine to Jonathan's luxury midtown
Toronto condominium. Past the doorman and up in
the lift, Cynthia found herself in a luxuriously carpeted
living-room with a view of the lake, an enclosed
courtyard outside with Jacuzzi and garden.

'You like hot pools?' she said when she saw it.

'Yes,' he said, 'but I'll like it better when you're in
it.' He reached for her and she went greedily into his
arms, the familiar need surging over her when his lips
found hers. When his hand slid down her back, she
moved in a way that she knew would disturb him.

His arms hardened. 'I'll cancel the meeting,' he said.

They both knew he couldn't. He'd already put off
the meeting in Vancouver once to steal a week with
her in Cabo San Lucas. His mouth moved to her throat
and as she melted against him he groaned, 'Be here
when I get back.'

'Yes,' she promised and, although he broke away
from her, her pulse was hammering with deep
satisfaction.

He studied her with laughter beneath his own frown. 'You look very pleased with yourself,' he teased softly.

'You'll be back,' she said. Her voice was a husky invitation because she'd learned in the last three days that she had an incredibly wild well of sensuality in her, her soul's answer to his passion.

'I'm tempted to kidnap you,' he muttered. 'Come to Vancouver with me.'

'I wish you could,' she whispered, but they both knew that she couldn't avoid her meeting tomorrow morning with the architects for the new subdivision. 'I wish I could throw out the architects and get you instead.'

'You'd have a lawsuit on your hands. Fax me the preliminaries tomorrow night and I'll have a look at them.' They'd already discussed this and in her suitcase she had a series of sketches which Jonathan had done of the ideas they'd developed for the community centre building at The Heights. She hugged the memory to herself. The original drawings had been developed in sand on the beach at Cabo and she'd felt the excitement of sharing her ideas and seeing Jonathan translate her semi-formed pictures of how it should be into visible lines on sand.

'I'll show you where everything is,' he said now, and it was a quick tour. Twenty minutes he'd stolen to introduce her to her new Toronto home. They'd stolen extra hours this morning in Cabo San Lucas before they'd left the hotel, so time was short now.

'I'll miss you,' she said and she almost added the other words. *I love you*. The words burned in her whenever he was near.

'I already miss *you*.' His eyes caressed her and she told herself that every look, every word he spoke was his way of saying he loved her. Not with a declaration but with every action and the words hidden underneath.

Then he was gone and she was prowling the condominium, knowing she should be getting ready for tomorrow's meeting with the architects. Soon she would take a taxi to the house she'd lived in before Jonathan. She needed to pack a few things, including her papers on the subdivision. She would arrange for the rest of her personal things to be brought here by movers.

As for the furniture — there wasn't much she would keep. She wouldn't keep the house either. It was tied to the past, to the empty years when she was playing the public part of Eric's wife while she lived in private isolation. The past was gone. Jonathan was right. There was only the future, and she hugged it to herself as she walked through the modern luxury of his apartment.

'We'll get rid of it if you don't want to live here,' he'd said with a casual gesture that swept the luxurious beauty aside. 'Or keep it for convenience in the city and build a country retreat.' And as she walked through the rooms she thought that yes, they would build a country retreat.

If only there could be children. . .

She pushed that away. She had enough of her dreams now. 'We can adopt,' he'd said, and perhaps that was what they would do. Children running through the rolling hills of a country retreat. With Jonathan's helicopter and all the conveniences of modern transportation there was no need to live in the city.

She stopped in the middle of his garden and looked out at the tall buildings in the distance. Jonathan's jet would have taken off by now. He was on his way to the west coast and she wished she could have gone with him.

If it weren't for Dyson Holdings she could.

He would be five days on the west coast. Too long. If she could settle the business with the architect tomorrow and plough her way through the paperwork waiting downtown, she could fly to him. She hugged herself and let anticipation spread through her. Twenty-four hours and she could be on her way to Jonathan!

When she got to Vancouver she would talk to him about Dyson Holdings. She'd focused all her energies on Dyson for years because there was nothing else in her life. Now there was Jonathan, and it was crazy to let chains from the past keep them apart. She'd finish The Heights project, but then she'd find a way to get out of management of Dyson.

She grimaced because one day soon the minority shareholders would be on her back. Two years ago when Allan had sold the last of his Dyson shares, she hadn't been able to buy them herself. They'd gone through a broker and it was only luck that the new owners hadn't challenged her position as general manager. She hadn't been making the kind of profit her father had. She'd gone into low-income housing and, if the accountants could be believed, Dyson's net worth had decreased over the years she'd had control.

Her fault, but money wasn't everything. That was what she'd told the chief accountant, but she'd known the minority shareholders could make it tough for her to take on more low-income housing projects. Luckily, the biggest of the minorities had voted by proxy at the last two annual general meetings, and Cynthia had stayed in power.

Jonathan would know ways to do the kind of things she'd been wanting to do without losing money. Jonathan could keep the minority shareholders quiet forever and still build day-cares and community recreation complexes. She'd talk to him about finding a new general manager for Dyson. She'd take a seat on the board and they would hire a manager. Then she'd be free to go where her husband went.

She hurried back into the living-room and picked up the antique telephone there. She travelled enough that she knew the travel agent's number by heart, and in two minutes she had a reservation on tomorrow's late flight to Vancouver.

She would surprise Jonathan. Tomorrow night, and she had a key to the Vancouver apartment. She laughed because he'd given her keys to an assortment of places yesterday. Vancouver and Paris and Toronto. Keys to his life, but there wasn't a country retreat in the lot unless you counted the island in the Mediterranean.

They would build their country home together.

'Jonathan Halley,' said the architect when she handed him the drawings for the modifications to the day-care plans. 'Only Halley could create elegant utility in a day-care centre. Ever since I read the news about your marriage —— ' He frowned. 'Are you planning to replace us with Halley on this contract?'

'No,' she said.

Jonathan had phoned her at dawn today from Vancouver and they'd talked briefly about this meeting. . .a couple of sentences squeezed between the important things — like Jonathan missing her and Cynthia asking if they could plan a new home together. 'But I would like those changes made,' she said, and she knew from the look the architect gave her that her colour was high with memories of that early-morning phone conversation.

'Right,' agreed the architect. 'And I suppose there will be other changes as we go on?'

'I'd like you to co-ordinate with my husband on these

plans.' *My husband.* Saying the words sent a shiver of warmth deep inside. 'Do you have a problem with that?'

He shook his head. 'I don't have a problem with it. Halley's ideas are always the sort of thing that make the rest of us wonder why the hell we didn't think of them first.' He gestured towards the plans. 'I hope some of his genius will rub off on me.'

Jonathan would laugh at that. She'd tell him tonight and he'd shrug off the comment about genius because he wasn't arrogant. He was. . .Jonathan. Her Jonathan.

She called her office before she left the architect's office.

'Sandra? I'm going to stop for lunch then I'll be in.'

When Sandra said, 'Fine, Mrs Halley,' Cynthia heard her married name as if it were a caress directly from Jonathan. She was glad she'd never taken Eric's name during their cool marriage. It made her using Jonathan's name more meaningful. It said to the world that she belonged to Jonathan Halley, even though she hadn't had the nerve yet to tell him how much she loved him.

On her way out of the restaurant after lunch she paused at the display window of a small boutique. The evening dress in the window. . .long and elegant and high-cut at the front with a dramatic simplicity. It had no back at all and she shivered as she stared at it. If she wore that dress with her hair falling to her waist, Jonathan's eyes would flare with desire. And when they danced she would feel her hair drifting over her naked back and Jonathan's hands on her flesh.

There was no price-tag on the dress. Just the designer's name and she knew it would be an outrageous price. It was insane to spend that much money on one dress.

She knew she would buy it. She had tickets to a charity ball here in Toronto in three weeks' time. She'd planned to ask Allan to go with her, but now it would be Jonathan at her side. Her lover; the man she lived with. Her husband. When she came out of their bedroom wearing that dress he would freeze, motionless except for his eyes. He would kiss her naked shoulder and she would shudder with desire. All evening, whenever he looked at her in the midst of the crowd, she would know that afterwards. . .

She paid for it by cheque, using the first cheque in the cheque-book she'd been given yesterday when Jonathan made a twenty-minute stop with her at his bank on the way to the condominium.

'I don't need this,' she'd said when she saw how much money he'd transferred to her account.

'Then don't spend it,' he'd suggested. But he'd smiled then and said, 'But I wish you would. If there's anything you want that I can give you, then I want you to have it.'

Jonathan's wife. Writing the cheque was an act of acceptance of that role. She would be Jonathan's wife for the rest of her life. Jonathan's forever, and he hadn't told her that he loved her with words, but everything he did spoke for him. All she would ever have to do to feel him near was to call his name or lift a telephone or use his cheque-book to buy a ticket to wherever he was.

Tonight she would fly to him. She'd hung up the phone this morning on his promise to call early the next morning. But she would see him before tomorrow morning. She was taking the midnight flight, and because of the time change she'd be in Vancouver at one in the morning. He was cramming a week's work into five days so that he'd be back to her quickly. He'd probably still be up, reading plans under the light of a lamp. She'd open the door with her new key and walk in. He'd look up at her and there would be pleasure and surprise in his eyes. Then he would put the construction plans aside as if they were waste paper and he'd stand up and come to her.

If she didn't stop this she'd never get through any work! She'd be in her office until at least eight tonight as it was, but with all this daydreaming she'd have to take a case full of papers with her on the plane trip to Jonathan. She didn't want that. She wanted it all behind her and only Jonathan on her mind.

Sandra met her as she came into the office. 'Welcome back, Mrs Halley. Congratulations!'

Cynthia flushed and said, 'I'm still Cynthia.' She saw Sandra's eyes flick to the door of Cynthia's office and then she noticed the discreet new sign there.

'Cynthia Dyson-Paige Halley.'

She laughed then because the world was only roses now. 'What a mouthful!' she said, but she would use his name. That was how it was on the new cheques and that was who she would be. Cynthia Halley. She'd leave the past behind and walk straight into the future at Jonathan's side.

'Are you ready for the uproar?' asked Sandra. 'The phone's been ringing off the hook. The magazines want interviews. The local dailies too.'

'Fend them off,' she said.

'All sorts of articles about you and Mr Halley,' said Sandra. 'You may have seen some of them?'

She shook her head. 'I've been in Mexico. Haven't looked at a newspaper in a week.' She flushed at the look of understanding in Sandra's eyes and then she laughed. What did it matter if the world knew how she felt about Jonathan?

Sandra spread her hands wide. 'They've been digging into corporate structures and old records. I had

Emersons start a clipping file in case you wanted it.'
She gestured towards the closed door to Cynthia's
office. 'I didn't know you'd been involved with him so
long.' Sandra flushed. 'Sorry, I know it's not my
business. I just couldn't help reading some of it and—
the clippings are on your desk.'

The public record of her romance with Jonathan?
Sandra didn't know the half of the real story. Neither
did the newsmen. No one but she and Jonathan knew,
but she supposed they'd all had their guesses.

'I'll be in my office,' she said. 'Don't put any calls
through unless they're from my husband.'

She went into the office and closed the door on what
had once been her father's sanctum. She looked around
and decided that she didn't like it much. She wasn't
sure she ever had. She'd kept the old décor and she
supposed she'd felt some sort of victory at sitting in his
old chair. As if she were the one who had won their
battle in the end. A sour victory, because she wasn't
interested in this empire and maybe she never had
been. It had been a way of asserting her personality
over her father's harsh dominance. She thought he
hadn't been so much like that before her mother died.

She thought of losing Jonathan and she shuddered
because that had happened once, and maybe she could
understand how losing a love could take the love out
of life. For the first time she felt pity for her father
because that must be what had happened to him. Pray
God she'd have years and years before there was a
chance of being parted from the man *she* loved.

Until death. . .

That was the only thing that could take him from
her.

He'd said that he hadn't been with another woman
since he learned that she was free. It was four years
since Eric had died. Four years and she'd seen

Jonathan several times. She'd tried not to look for him
at charity balls; she had been caught by his eyes across
the heads of faceless people. What if she'd stepped
towards him instead of away at one of those public
events they'd shared? Would he have pursued her
then?

He'd had no other women once he knew she was
free. That had to mean that he'd loved her forever,
that he'd never turn her away, never——

No! No more of the past. Only the future. She
wouldn't spoil the wonder of her love trying to understand old pains. Old betrayals. If it happened again—
if he betrayed her now when her whole existence was
consumed with loving him——

She shivered and tried to shake the fear away, to
think of how he'd been when he left her. Of how his
voice had rumbled in her ear this morning when she'd
reached for the ringing telephone on the bedside table.

'You're still in my bed,' he'd said. 'You sound all
sleepy.'

'Mm,' she'd murmured, and with her eyes closed
she'd imagined that he was there on the other side of
this bed where she'd spent the night dreaming of him.
'All alone in bed,' she'd said.

He'd laughed, and then he'd said something that had
made her pulse hammer.

If she could talk to Jonathan now she would feel
better. The fears would recede. They weren't rational
fears. If she focused on the Jonathan of the last few
days and didn't let herself remember how he'd once
stared at her as if he hated her, there wouldn't be any
reason to fear. Fourteen years ago. Too far back to
matter.

She reached for the telephone. She would call him.
His voice would push back her insecurities. He'd called
her at dawn—four in the morning on the west coast.

He'd been sleepless, thinking of her, wishing she were with him. It was this office making her afraid. The seat of her father's old empire had brought the past back. Her father's voice saying, 'Stay away from that Halley kid' and Jonathan himself saying, 'Get out of here' — only in her mind it had echoed as if he had said it today.

Jonathan's secretary answered the telephone. 'Oh, Mrs Halley!' she said warmly. Two weeks ago she'd seemed iron-grey and hard, but now Evelyn Shandrom's voice was warm and co-operative. 'I'm afraid he's just gone out. He's meeting with a delegation from city council. He'll be back at three — ah, six in the evening your time. Shall I ask him to call you?'

'Yes,' she said, 'please do, Evelyn. Tell him I'll still be at the office.'

Of course he couldn't be there every time she called. She understood that. She picked up a clipping from the pile Sandra had left on her desk and stared at a picture of her and Jonathan together — the picture taken at the airport in Vancouver as they were leaving on their honeymoon.

SURPRISE MERGER — HALLEY AND DYSON-PAIGE.

Merger! What a headline! What a way to put it, as if she and Jonathan had married for business reasons. She smiled a little because they would never know that it had started that way, an affair of marriage for money. That would make a horrifying headline. HALLEY AND DYSON-PAIGE — MARRIAGE FOR MONEY. But it hadn't stayed that way. Jonathan had torn up the contract within an hour of marrying her.

All her life she'd been used as a pawn. By her father. By Eric McAulisson. Even, she supposed, by Allan. But not Jonathan. He'd torn up his power over her as if *she* mattered more.

She put the speculative article aside and picked up the next one.

The journalists had done a lot of guesswork. She scanned four or five articles and saw that the Press had discovered that they'd both lived in Parkland when they were children. She half expected to see an account of the car accident and she was ready to put that aside without reading it if she did. Jonathan was right. The past was over.

There was no reference to the accident in the articles she looked at. She supposed the reporters had searched records of births and deaths and old newspaper articles, but that was all. She knew her father would have used his influence to keep any mention of Allan's accident out of the papers.

Someone had found a picture of her father's funeral. Jonathan and Cynthia standing together, and somehow the cameraman had taken it at an angle that made it look as if they were talking intimately. Jonthan's hand had been lifted as if about to touch her shoulder with sympathy and support. She hadn't known that there was a camera there, and in that moment she probably wouldn't have noticed a flash bulb going off in her eyes. She and Jonathan had been fighting—or she'd been fighting and he'd been watching, because Jonathan wasn't a man who got involved in futile battles. She'd never seen Jonathan in a rage except that once when she was sixteen and he went up to her house to confront her father. And even then the rage had been leashed in with cold determination.

She should be working.

She was going to get out of this office, out of this business. She'd work on the day-care for The Heights, and that was all. From there on she'd work with Jonathan. He'd asked her yesterday if she might want to work with him on the community facilities for a

convalescent centre he'd been asked to design in
Switzerland. Her ideas, and he would translate them
into walls and spaces. It would be fun working with
Jonathan. She looked around her office and wondered
why she'd wanted control of her father's old empire,
but she knew the answer. She'd needed something to
do desperately when she'd discovered the truth about
her marriage to Eric. And once her father died someone had to take over and Allan hadn't been interested.

Now she could be free of it.

She ruffled through her messages. She'd better do
these first, return the calls to the estate agent who was
arranging the sublet of the commercial development at
The Heights, and the accountant who wanted her to go
over the interim financial statements.

She pushed the clippings aside. She would take them
with her. Jonathan might like to see them. She would
keep the photos of Jonathan and the one from the
airport, with Jonathan looking down at her as if he'd
just won something he'd wanted all his life.

The word 'takeover' caught her eyes and she pulled
back the pile of clippings. HALLEY TAKEOVER OF DYSON
HOLDINGS COMPLETE.

She made a sound of disgust. Some reporters could
make anything seem shady. She smoothed out the page
where it had been folded and her gaze fell to the first
paragraph.

Jonathan Halley has a growing string of awe-
inspiring architectural structures to his credit, but
the architect may now be moving into a new area of
property development.

Two years ago Halley's Western Wave Enterprises
bought a significant minority interest in Dyson
Holdings, the empire founded by entrepreneur
Samuel Dyson. With the marriage last week between

Halley and Cynthia Dyson-Paige, Halley and
Western Wave now have effective control over the
high-risk Dyson.

Dyson has been involved in several unprofitable
enterprises since its founder's death five years ago,
but with Halley at the helm we should expect an
innovative and profitable new direction for Dyson
Holdings.

It wasn't true.

Western Wave Holdings. She stumbled to her feet.
Western Wave was the owner of those minority shares.
But it had to be a mistake. Jonathan didn't own
Western Wave.

She pulled open the top drawer of her filing-cabinet.
Shareholders' minutes. She opened the file folder and
a sheaf of papers spilled out. Nothing there except
what she knew already. Those shares had been voted
by proxy given to Dyson's lawyer.

Why would Jonathan want shares in her company?
There was no reason for him to do that. No reason at
all. It wasn't true. Jonathan would have told her.

If it was true. . .

She reached for the telephone and dialled her lawyer's office.

'Congratulations,' Ken Olterham said warmly. 'I'm
very happy for you, Cynthia. I've been meaning to call
you — didn't know if you'd be back from your honeymoon yet.'

'Thanks, Ken.' It would be all right. A mistake.
Reporters got things mixed up all the time. 'Ken, can
you look up the last proxy for the Western Wave shares
and see who signed it?'

'Sure. Hold on, I've got the file here.'

She waited and as each second ticked past she came
closer to knowing it would be all right. A mistake.

Reporters made mistakes all the time, but this one was a real fairy-tale.

'Got it,' said Ken. 'Signed by the secretary-treasurer.'

'Yes,' she said, but her heart had slowed now. She shouldn't have panicked, shouldn't have doubted Jonathan so easily. Guilt warred with dying fear.

'E. Shandrom,' Ken said.

'No,' she whispered, but she felt everything crumbling. Evelyn Shandrom. Jonathan's personal assistant.

There was only one reason for Jonathan's personal assistant to have her name on that proxy. Because Jonathan wanted a name to take an inconspicuous place on the proxy, a name Cynthia wouldn't suspect had anything to do with him. His personal assistant was a natural choice. An obvious way to deceive Cynthia, except that now they were married. Now Jonathan's office was part of her life and Evelyn's name a household word.

Hadn't he realised that she would be talking to Evelyn all the time, that the name would strike her as if it were Jonathan's hand slapping across her face?

The telephone rang under her hand. She jerked away from it.

Jonathan.

It rang again.

She fled to the window. Her body jerked with each ring. Evelyn Shandrom. She was fortyish and efficient, probably married to her job.

Western Wave belonged to Jonathan, a front for his investment in her company. Jonathan taking over her life piece by piece and Allan had made it easy. Those shares he'd dumped in a private offering at a Toronto brokerage two years ago. Then that promissory note. Jonathan owned Dyson Holdings and he owned

Cynthia and, if she thought she'd been used before, this made past betrayals look like nothing.

Jonathan had used everything against her. Her loyalty to her brother. Her desire to prove that she could manage her father's empire successfully. Her old love for Jonathan Halley.

He'd used her. He'd made her love him again and he'd used that, too.

She looked around at the office and wondered what it was that Jonathan wanted here. She would have given it to him, had decided to ask him to take it off her hands. If that article had stayed in obscurity for another week, Jonathan's man would have been in here and Cynthia would have willingly stepped back.

She'd been so damned naïve she hadn't even suspected he had any motive other than wanting her. Loving her. Fool! He'd *never* said he loved her! She'd made that fantasy up as if she were a dreaming child. No different than the fantasies she'd had when he used to talk to her when she was a kid. She'd been a sucker for Jonathan all her life and he had to know that.

He must have laughed when she said she wouldn't consummate their marriage. He'd known all along that he could make a fool of her whenever he chose!

Someone tapped on her door.

She ignored it.

The phone rang again and she didn't answer that either. She didn't want any calls put through except her husband's, she'd told Sandra. No calls but Jonathan's, and he would be returning her call now. She'd wanted him to reassure her that her doubts were groundless.

Evelyn would have given him her message. Call your wife.

Eveyln who had signed the proxy for Western Wave.

CHAPTER NINE

CYNTHIA boarded the jet just before midnight. She took only a light holdall because she wouldn't be gone long. She needed only enough time to tell Jonathan Halley what she thought of him.

She held her anger tight all through the flight. The in-flight movie was an adventure film full of violence and killing. She told herself that she'd like to be the one behind the gun; that she wished Jonathan Halley had never been born. That she felt nothing except a cold knot of anger and she wanted it that way.

He wasn't at his penthouse apartment. She unlocked the door with the key he'd given her, and when it swung open it banged against the stop because she'd pushed hard. But he wasn't there. He wasn't sitting in a chair reading plans or sleeping in the big bed down the hallway. Heaven knew where he was and she didn't care.

She sat on the sofa and she didn't move much until it was dawn. She felt dizzy when she got up. She forced herself to go into his kitchen and make herself a sandwich. She ate half of it and then she went out on to his patio and stared at the rising sun.

If he hadn't spent the night here then he was probably in Parkland. She turned around and she was still dizzy. She hadn't slept last night and it was three hours later by her internal clock than by the rising sun.

She went into his bathroom and washed her hands and face. She took her travel toothbrush out of her bag and brushed her teeth. Then she brushed out her hair

152

and put it back up in the knot Jonathan didn't like. She would wear it that way forever now.

She took her holdall with her when she left his apartment. She intended to rent a car but she would be a hazard behind the wheel until she cooled the anger and got some sleep. She took a taxi to the bus depot, then the bus to the ferry terminal.

It was ten in the morning when she got to the yellow and white construction trailer. Work had progressed here while Jonathan had been deceiving her. There were walls on top of the foundation; the building was growing, drowning out her old home. She stopped outside the trailer and took a deep breath before she opened the door. Then she pushed it open quickly and stepped inside.

Empty.

Last time there had been several men. Jonathan had been laughing until he saw her. He'd already owned a big chunk of her company then. He'd been holding the investment. Waiting.

This time there was no one. She turned blindly back to the door and then she saw him. He came up the stairs and through the open door as she reached for it.

'Where the hell have you been?' he demanded.

He was reaching for her until she backed away from him, until she screamed, 'Don't touch me! Don't you ever touch me again!'

The lines of his face shifted from tension to granite. He gave the door a push. It slammed closed behind him.

'Right,' he said grimly. 'What's this about?'

'What do you think?' she demanded. She forced herself to stand her ground when every instinct screamed at her to back away from him. 'How much of a fool do you think I am? Did you think I'd never find out?'

'What in hell are you going on about?' He ran one hand through his hair. 'I've been calling you since yesterday afternoon. Your secretary hasn't a clue where you are. Neither has Allan.' The granite aged suddenly and he said, 'You haven't been heard of in any of Toronto's hospitals. The doorman at the condo says you were in and gone again before midnight. Carrying a bag.'

She made a brittle sound like a laugh. 'You're good at keeping track of me, aren't you? Keep track. . .keep control.' She reached into her pocket and pulled out a sheaf of papers. 'Or do you just *buy* control?'

'You're not making a lot of sense.'

'This is all of it,' she said wildly. She shoved the papers into his hands. 'The shares. The rest of Dyson Holdings. That's what you wanted, isn't it? First you bought Allan's share when he sold——' She waved the share certificates wildly. 'Oh, you did a lovely job of fooling me about that! Evelyn's name on the proxy and you hiding behind a damned holding company! Because the whole damned world knew it was you— every bloody business reporter in the country knew who *really* bought those shares! But not *me*! When I came to *you* for help I hadn't a clue—had no idea then what you really wanted! Well, there it is! Take them, why don't you? Every damned share is yours, bought and paid for!'

He didn't take the papers and she dropped them and stormed across the trailer to the window, then spun back immediately to face him. He hadn't moved from the door, but she felt as if he was crawling up on her from behind. She could hear the echo of her voice, high and sounding more like hysteria than fury, but she couldn't stop the words.

'I thought you were different! You're no different!

You bought me and paid for me and that damned contract was the worst irony of all!'

He picked up the share certificates. He folded them carefully where they had been folded before. Then he stepped forward and she backed against the window but he stopped at the counter where he dropped the certificates.

'There is no contract,' he said flatly. His eyes were black with no lights flaring in them. 'The only contract between us is our marriage.'

Her laugh went up the scales like a soprano out of control. 'Oh, yes! Of course you tore it up! That was safe enough, wasn't it? Because you knew I could never forget it! You made me think you weren't trying to push me around and all the time it was the biggest betrayal of all! You had me in a little box and you just watched while I ran on the treadmill!' She was screaming, gulping air and the words tumbling out louder and sharper. 'You tricked me! No obligation, you said! You knew I'd fall for that!' She squeezed her eyes closed and hissed, 'You even told me it was strategy. And I still fell for it. Damn you!'

She opened her eyes and nothing had changed. His face was harsh and shuttered and she'd let herself forget this part of him. She'd let him seduce her into *asking* him to make love to her. She'd let the sex and her own crazy dreams blind her to this side of the man.

'Aren't you going to say *anything*? Don't you have anything at all to say?'

'You're doing a fine job of saying it all. I imagine they can hear you over in Vancouver. What do you want me to add?' He slid one hand into his jacket pocket. 'If you believe I've been plotting against you, tricking you out of these——' he thumped his hand down on the share certificates '—then perhaps you can explain to me what my motive is supposed to be?'

She shuddered because it was the past all over again. Jonathan who had acted as if he loved her. He was staring at her as if she were crawling under a microscope.

'I should have known,' she whispered. 'You wrecked my car with Allan in it and you didn't give a damn about him. You said you owed him nothing and I don't know how I could have let myself hear that and not realise that nothing could ever change.'

She could hear her own breathing, could feel her chest aching with explosive bursts of the air she forced into it. Jonathan said nothing and she wasn't sure she'd hear if he did speak. Her ears were roaring and her blood pounding hard.

'I'm leaving you,' she said. 'Divorce me for desertion if you want. I'm calling the bloody papers and everyone will know that there's no marriage, no—nothing.'

He made a slashing motion with his free hand. She jerked as if he'd threatened her. 'I'll see you in hell before I divorce you,' he growled. She gasped and he said, 'If you want to run then start moving but I'm damned if I'll lift my little finger to make it easier for you.'

She glared at him and he glared back. Then the door opened and someone started to come in.

'Get out!' snapped Jonathan, and the door slammed closed with a bang.

She was glad she'd poked hard enough to see fury raging in Jonathan's eyes like hate, his body coiled and tight as if only a thread stopped him throttling her. This was how she would remember him. The last time, when she'd left him on that porch, she'd been aching and yearning. But this time it was dead. She looked at him and she couldn't even remember how it had felt to need him so badly that she was ready to beg for his love.

'If you're leaving,' he said grimly, 'I'd suggest you wait long enough to take what you wanted the last time.'

She didn't love him. She'd never loved him. She'd made a man in her mind and loved the image. Not this creature with his face hard and brutal, his voice a weapon that slashed along her nerves.

'Allan's promissory note. It's in my safe in Vancouver.'

The promissory note. The money.

She closed her eyes and Jonathan's damned money was all around her.

'Damn you,' she whispered. Her shares in Dyson were lying on that counter but by no stretch of her imagination would they cover the amount of that damned note. She opened her eyes and saw Jonathan's face, and in his eyes the trap she could never escape.

'All right,' she said dully. She could feel the anger draining from her and leaving emptiness. 'All right. I——'

'Cynthia, you can't——'

She flung out a hand to ward off his touch. 'No! Don't—don't you! I made a deal.' She had to keep swallowing because something was choking her. 'I signed it—I signed and—— You tore up that contract, but I intend to live by every clause in it. I'll live under your roof.' She swallowed air and said, 'When you're in Parkland I'll be in Toronto. Under your roof. When you're in Toronto I'm going to the Mediterranean.' She clenched her jaw and said raggedly, 'I always wanted to occupy an island in the Mediterranean. But *not with you.*'

'Call my secretary for my schedule,' he suggested. 'I plan to do a lot of travelling. If you want to avoid me you'll have your work cut out.'

'You're standing in my way.' There was a pain

growing deep inside her stomach. Maybe she had ulcers or maybe screaming hurt something at the core of a person's body. 'Let me out of here. I want out.'

He stepped aside and she dodged around him. At the door she clenched her fingers on the handle. 'I'll have a copy made of the contract,' she said, fighting the nausea inside. 'I'll fax it to you. You'd better read it again because I'm holding you to every clause.'

He smiled and it wasn't pleasant. 'Including the one about consummating the marriage? No consummation unless you ask, but there's nothing in there about who sleeps where on the nights after the consummation.'

'Bastard,' she hissed. She turned the handle of the door and jerked it open.

'I'll send you to Vancouver in the helicopter.'

'No, thanks! I'll find my own way.'

'Shall I increase your allowance for the extra plane fares? You'll be doing a lot of travelling avoiding me.'

'I'm not spending your damned money!' She remembered the designer gown she'd bought and she shuddered. She'd pay him back. She'd get the bloody money back in the account before he knew. Then she'd——

'You've already spent a pile,' he reminded her. 'On your brother.'

'I'm getting out of here! It starts now! You're here and I'm damned well leaving. You once told me there was nothing in the past for us! Maybe there isn't anything for you, but there is for me! The past isn't over and it never was, and I'm not going to forget one word of what happened between you and me! Not ever again!'

He reached out and gripped her arm. She froze and stared at his hand on her. 'Are you into force now, Jonathan? Is that what you do when manipulation won't work?'

'Remember it all,' he said harshly. 'When you're

remembering, don't forget that you begged me to be your lover and that you told me two days ago you couldn't remember a time when you'd been happier. Remember it all because it's all in there, moon lady. Every damned minute of it.'

She jerked away from his touch and ran down the stairs away from him.

Jonathan knew he'd made a mistake the moment Cynthia opened the door. Three weeks and he was getting desperate, but he knew it wouldn't work even before she opened the door.

She was dressed in a gold satin jacket that dropped dramatically from a high neckline to mid-thigh. She was expecting him, perhaps even expecting that he would be early. She didn't say hello when she opened the door. Brown trousers under the golden jacket, golden high-heels. It was a costume, as dramatic and as cold as the anger in her eyes.

She had her hair up.

'I'm ready,' she said. She picked up a gold bag that matched the jacket.

He glanced at his watch deliberately. 'We're early,' he said although he knew there was no point. She wouldn't be dressed like that if she had any intention of this being anything but a cold evening.

His apartment, but if he went in she'd go out of the door in the same breath. It had been like that for three weeks. He'd come to Toronto three days after she'd raged at him at the Parkland construction site. He'd been waiting in the living-room when she'd come home from her office. She'd frozen to ice the instant she realised he was there, then she'd walked into the bedroom.

He'd followed, and watched her pack a small case.

He'd caught one second of emotion in her eyes when she'd looked up at him just after the case was closed.

'You should have asked Evelyn for my schedule,' he'd snapped.

Then he'd seen her expression shutter, and knew that his words had hurt her somewhere inside where she wouldn't let him look. He'd realised an instant too late that if he'd said the right thing in that moment they might have been able to talk.

Damn his temper! He could hold on to it while talking to unions and environmentalists, so why couldn't he keep his cool when it was Cynthia, and losing it wasn't something he could even contemplate?

He knew the answer. Because everything else was a game and she had always been the real thing. He'd lost her once, and if he wasn't very careful he would lose her again.

He wasn't sure what would bring her closer and what would send her away and he seemed doomed to make mistakes with her. Like mentioning that damned note of Allan's when she was screaming at him in Parkland. If they had any chance at all it was only if they could put everything else aside. The shares and the note and the past, that hellish twenty-four hours that had begun when he'd stared at the ugly bruise that Samuel Dyson had inflicted on his daughter. Punishment for the magic that had flared between two kids; punishment for loving.

Losing her had been the only way to protect her. And now——

He was damned if he'd lose her again!

She was determined to keep the continent between them. When he'd come to Toronto she'd left within minutes. When he'd returned to Vancouver his doorman had told him Cynthia had been there for three days. She'd just left. He knew from Evelyn that she'd

got his schedule while she was in Vancouver and he
didn't need anyone to tell him that that was why she'd
left two hours before he'd arrived.

He could play the game, too. He'd left a message on
her answering machine demanding that she keep him
advised of her movements.

She'd countered by faxing his Vancouver apartment
with *her* schedule.

She was keeping to the letter of that agreement,
always under his roof but never in the same city. He'd
like to take that damned contract and stuff it down her
throat.

All right. She'd agreed to act as his wife in public, so
that was where they'd work their future out. In public.
He'd given her three weeks to wonder what would
come next. Then he'd faxed her a note stating that he
would escort her to the Niderstrom charity ball on the
twenty-second of May. She'd faxed back that she would
be ready for him to pick her up at eight in the evening.

The next day Alicia had dropped into the Vancouver
office. He'd taken her to lunch but he was in no mood
to have patience with his sister's bad temper.

'I called your wife,' Alicia announced. 'I said I
wanted to give a reception for her.' She glared at him.
'She wouldn't give me a date when she'd be in
Vancouver. Do you have any idea how I felt
when——?'

'Alicia!' All he needed was his well-intentioned but
militant sister throwing spanners into the works.
'Alicia,' he warned, 'back off.'

Her jaw hardened with the same stubbornness he
remembered from his old man. 'You shouldn't have
married her,' said Alicia. 'She's never been anything
but trouble. I know damned well there was something
funny about that accident — you and *her* brother. When
did you ever hang out with Allan Dyson-Paige? You

would never talk about it — you think I didn't know you were hiding something? You smashed up that car of hers? I don't believe it! You should never have let them pin the blame on you! It had to be because of *her*, because she begged you to bail out her stupid drunk of a brother! And now you're mixed up with her again and——'

'Alicia!' He pushed aside the plate between them. 'Stay out of this. I won't forgive you if you hurt Cynthia.'

'I've been polite,' she protested.

He leaned forward and said quietly, 'You're my sister and I love you, but she's my wife and if you do anything to her you're doing it to me, too. She knows you don't like her and I won't have it, Alicia. You can suspect what you want about the past but if you hurt Cynthia you'll be driving a permanent wedge between us because I *won't* let her be hurt.'

His sister's lips parted on a protest.

He shook his head sharply.

'She's taking advantage of you,' said Alicia.

He shook his head. 'No, she's not. I practically blackmailed her into marrying me. She's the only woman I've ever wanted and I'm gambling that I can win her, but it isn't over yet.'

Alicia picked up her fork and twisted it into a limp leaf of lettuce. 'You're telling me not to throw spanners in your works.'

'I'm telling you I won't let you.'

Truce with Alicia. If only it were as simple to deal with Cynthia.

The charity ball was the first step. He rang the bell of the Toronto condominium at six-thirty on the evening of the ball. An hour and a half early, and with luck he hoped Cynthia might decide to offer him a drink. Maybe they could talk. But then he saw her face and he knew it wasn't going to be that easy. He would need all the patience he could muster, but patience was getting harder and harder when he could see her slipping away from him.

'I'll take you to dinner first,' he said and she nodded agreement.

Over dinner she managed to keep up a bright dissertation on the guests who were expected to be at the ball.

'I don't give a damn who's coming,' he said when the waiter had delivered their coffee. 'I came to see you. No other reason.'

She closed her lips tightly and he realised that it was worse than he'd thought. She wouldn't even argue. He thought about transferring these bloody Dyson shares to her but had a feeling that would only make things worse. He should never have bought the shares; he wouldn't have touched them if he hadn't had dinner with Harry Trederson one night two years ago. After they'd agreed on a price for the land on the east coast, Trederson had confided that he'd picked up a significant minority interest in Dyson.

Jonathan had known the kind of pressure Trederson could put on Cynthia at a shareholders' meeting. The man was a shark. It might take a year or two, but if Cynthia didn't get the dividends up to the level Trederson demanded, she'd lose control of her own company. Jonathan had manged to keep abreast of enough of the details of Dyson's management over the years to know that there was no way Cynthia could pay the kind of dividends her father had. She would never be the underhanded opportunist her old man had been and Trederson wouldn't tolerate softness.

So he'd bought the shares. Trederson didn't particularly want to sell, but Jonathan was even more determined to buy when he realised that Trederson had plans for using his influence to get Dyson into a couple of his pet land deals.

A time bomb, his ownership of the Dyson shares. He should have told her that day when she'd come to ask him to bail Allan out of the latest mess, but she'd been worried enough then. Bankruptcy facing her, and no way out except coming to a man she'd vowed she'd never ask for help.

What a bloody mess! The only thing he had on his side was time.

She was his wife, but the only way he could see her was to start incurring a bunch of social obligations and demand that she accompany him.

The charity ball was the first such obligation and it was a disaster. Masses of tiny sandwiches and a mediocre band. He got her in his arms four times because she could hardly refuse to dance with her own husband, but she held herself stiffly each time and moved like a machine to the music. She talked brightly and she smiled a lot, but her eyes were empty and her gaze wouldn't hold his.

She kept a glass in her hand when she was at the table but when the waiter came to her the only thing she drank was mineral water. She wasn't taking even that chance of letting her guard down.

Afterwards, he told the limousine driver to go slowly and they crawled through Toronto while Jonathan watched his wife from the seat opposite in the dimly lit interior of the limo. The glass partition between them and the driver was up. They were about as alone as they were likely to be tonight.

'Are you intending to stay at the condo tonight?' Her voice was tight and indifferent. He suspected that the question had been in her mind all evening.

'Not if you're planning to leave,' he said. He waited

out a long silence, then added quietly, 'If I stayed, Cynthia, I could sleep in the guest-room.'

The silence was so long that he began to hope she might say yes. Then she shook her head. Not yet. He knew he could lose her if he tried to force his hand. She'd been pushed around too much in her life, used by her father and Allan and that calculating bastard she had married. He knew his only chance of winning lay in letting her choose.

He wanted her willing and loving him, not trapped by feelings of duty in regard to that damned money he'd used to bail Allan out of disaster.

He could feel the wariness in her. She'd been uneasy around him always. . .dating back to that painful good-bye on the porch of his father's house.

But she'd come to him. He'd watched her for years, telling himself it was over but feeling pain every time her body stiffened at the sight of him. But then she'd come to him.

OK, he'd thought. It would take time. He'd wait forever for the right moment if he had to. That was what he'd told himself when she'd agreed to marry him. He had believed then that they had all the time in the world.

He hadn't dreamed how hard it would be. Worse now, because he had the memory of how it could be — of his name on her lips and her warmth surrounding him, of her laughter, and the simple pleasure of her hand lying trusting in his grasp.

She had a shell around her like a suit of armour but he'd seen cracks in it. Awareness in her eyes. That catch in her voice. The way she held herself very stiffly when he was close enough to reach out and touch her.

'We can't go on like this forever,' he said.

An ultimatum. He knew it was the wrong tactic.

She moved her hand and he saw that she was

trembling. His body urged aggression. He knew the needs of her woman's body intimately. He knew where to touch and how to kiss her and he *knew* with primeval certainty that she would respond. In the space of sixty seconds in the shadows of this limousine he could turn her body's tension to flaming desire. The pounding in his bloodstream demanded that he advance. . .seduce. . .take her in the most basic way of a man and a woman. Prove to her that she could never be free of the chemistry between them.

A gamble.

A man would be crazy to gamble when he couldn't afford to lose. If Jonathan seduced Cynthia into lowering her barriers, he would gain only one night. With the morning that followed he could lose her forever.

'I know this can't go on,' she said in a low voice. 'I know it.'

He read the decision in her voice and his blood chilled. He'd counted on the basic force between them to stop her from leaving him. If she left——

He took in a deep ragged breath.

'We're not getting a divorce, Cynthia. We'll talk about the Dyson thing. We'll talk about. . .about us.' He gestured in the general direction of the Dyson Holdings offices. 'The Dyson shares are yours. I never wanted them.'

'I don't want the damned shares,' she muttered.

'Cynthia——' Maybe it was the dim lighting in the limo but she looked too pale. Exhausted where she'd been tight with brittle energy back at that charity ball. He wanted to tell her to rest, to let him carry her up to her bed. He wanted to offer to leave her alone in the bedroom if only she would let him be close by, in the next room, even in the same city.

He made a frustrated gesture without words.

If he could sweep all this nonsense of money and

corporate manoeuvring aside they might have a chance. It had been simple in Cabo San Lucas. Just Cynthia and Jonathan, and without the obstacles she hadn't been able to deny that they belonged to each other.

'I never meant to do anything with Dyson,' he said. 'I just wanted to keep it out of unfriendly hands when Allan dumped the shares.' He made a frustrated sound deep in his throat. 'It's yours. I never intended anything else.'

She pushed her hand through the hair above her ear and an assortment of dark chestnut strands shone free in the dim light. 'Put a manager in. Do what you want with it. I don't care. All I want is the project at The Heights. Let me finish that and you can ——' She waved a hand vaguely and he realised that she wasn't meeting his eyes. 'Do whatever you want,' she finished.

'I want you.'

She shook her head.

'You're tired,' he said. 'It's too late for this.' The limousine stopped and he said abruptly, 'Get some sleep. I'll come back in the morning and we'll have breakfast and talk about—whatever it is we have to talk about.'

Later, when she could look at him without exhaustion written in every line of her body, he would ask what it was that she wanted. If he could manage to negotiate land deals with unenthusiastic vendors, surely he could find a compromise that could allow her to let her guard against him down again.

'We'll settle this business about the Dyson shares,' he vowed.

The driver opened the door.

Cynthia said, 'I suppose you had a reason for buying the shares. It doesn't matter. I don't care.' He saw her eyes close as she said, 'I was going to ask you to help me find a general manager to take my place. I wanted free of it anyway.'

'Cynthia——'

'I'm tired.'

'Leave us alone,' he murmured to the driver. He climbed out of the limo, then reached down his hand to help Cynthia out. She came to her feet only inches away from him and for a moment they were frozen together. It would have taken only the lightest pull of his hand to bring her into his arms.

He forced his body to step back when he heard her small whimper of protest. He reached out and touched her chin and her eyes came up but there wasn't enough light to read her emotions.

'If this isn't about Dyson Holdings, then what? Why won't you let me love you, moon lady?'

She drew her lip between her teeth. Without her consent, his fingertips stroked the length of her throat. If she didn't step away from him soon he would tangle his fingers in the smooth knot of her hair and when the waves came down around her shoulders he would pull her into his arms and they would both be lost.

'It's about trust,' she whispered.

He found only dark shadows in her eyes. He wondered what he would see if he had light. The pale white of her eyelids came down over her eyes and her voice filled with pain.

'Jonathan—it's about your not trusting me enough to explain what happened fourteen years ago. It's about——' She gasped and he realised that his hand had tightened on hers painfully.

'Don't throw us away for that.' He heard the harshness in his voice and tried to soften it because she was staring at him as if he'd frightened her.

She pulled back. 'I can't forget,' she said. Her voice was low and he knew this wasn't something he could change. She wasn't meeting his eyes with challenge. She wasn't fighting his will with hers.

'What can't you forget?'

'I thought you loved me.' He had to strain to hear her voice. 'You never said the words but I would have sworn——' She gestured blindly. 'Then you looked at me and I was nothing. Between one day and the next— between one breath and the next whatever you felt for me died. I can't forget that. I want to forget it. You said to leave the past but how can I forget that everything between us just crumbled into dust and I don't know why?'

He thought she sobbed and he reached for her but she backed away towards the building with her hands outspread as if to ward off a danger. 'You remember and I remember but you won't talk about it! You call me by the same name you called me then—moon lady! And I want—I wish—— How can I be your lady if you won't let me understand?'

'Don't leave,' he said but she was running from him.

He watched her go through the door and the night went darker.

CHAPTER TEN

ALL her dreams had turned to nightmares. Cynthia stood in Jonathan's garden staring at the city lights and she didn't know where to go or what she could do now.

He had an explanation for Dyson. She could have listened but she knew that that was only a hurdle between them and not the real problem. None of it made sense. He must have bought the Dyson shares for her. Not to interfere, but to protect her from an unfriendly takeover.

But why? He'd sent her away, told her to go when she was sixteen. 'Get out,' he'd said. Then, years later, he'd bought a big block of her family's company and now he said he'd done it for her. Throwing away his money, and he'd thrown more when she'd asked him to bail out Allan.

It would make sense if he loved her. If he'd always loved her.

She'd seen him over the years. Even when she was married to Eric, Jonathan had sometimes turned up at social events where she was present. Years of glimpses of the man who had taught her that love couldn't be trusted. Their eyes had locked whenever they'd met in public and she'd stared at him and been determined not to be the one to look away first, not to let him see that it still hurt.

Whenever she saw him she went home afterwards and told herself how she'd enjoyed the evening. She would catalogue all the people there and Jonathan's name would hardly be present in her mind. As if she hadn't noticed him.

She'd buried Jonathan's memory deep inside herself, but she'd never forgotten. When Allan had pushed her to the edge of bankruptcy and there was nowhere to turn, Jonathan's had been the first name in her mind. As if he'd been waiting there in her subconscious all those years. And when he'd told her his terms —

Marriage. Jonathan always near her. Always close.

Her body had known that she loved him. Even the infertility that the doctors had judged absolute had given way to Jonathan.

Jonathan Halley's baby was growing inside her now, and he said they couldn't go on like this. She knew he was right, knew she had to put the past behind her. But, although she willed herself to seal off the memories as if they'd never happened, the fear was there. Always waiting.

She wanted to trust him. She told herself that she could, that the past was past, but her fears betrayed her. Why wouldn't he talk about the past?

Acting as if he loved her for a magical week in Mexico. . .yet refusing to explain that old betrayal. He'd told her to forget the past, but the past was between them with every breath, every touch. Why would he pursue her so patiently through these last few weeks if he didn't love her? Why buy Dyson's shares and sit on them?

No reason if he didn't love her.

Why pay Allan's note when he said he didn't owe Allan a damned thing?

The night sounds flowed in around her and suddenly the world shifted and she was looking at it all from a different angle.

Why did he say he owed Allan nothing? It wasn't like the Jonathan she knew to dodge responsibility. He didn't make excuses. If Jonathan had been driving when that accident happened —

If——

If Jonathan had been driving.

With the night-time scent of Jonathan's garden in her nostrils she felt the past flow back. Watching Jonathan and her father on the steps of her house. They'd been shouting at each other and she'd run because it had terrified her. Her father had terrified her and she'd never seen Jonathan angry like that, couldn't face his anger because anger meant danger.

Then the accident. The explosion. Jonathan and Allan. She'd believed they were dead. She'd waited hours, with Mrs Corveson hovering. Waited to hear the words that would take Jonathan and her brother from her forever. Then the dawn, and she'd hardly heard what her father said about Jonathan being to blame and herself being sent to Switzerland. She'd only thought of Jonathan and when she'd stood there on his porch and he'd looked at her with coldness in his eyes she'd been devastated by his betrayal of her love. . . too hurt to question anything.

In all the years that followed, her memory of that twenty-four hours hinged on the instant when Jonathan had told her that he wouldn't wait for her. Jonathan who had touched her shoulder so gently that it soothed the pain. Jonathan who had asked her to come away with him because he couldn't let her be hurt again. Jonathan who had looked at her with hardness in his heart and said no, he wasn't waiting for her and she should get out of his life. Go to Switzerland.

Jonathan who hadn't touched another woman from the day he learned she was a widow.

He *had* waited.

She wasn't looking at it correctly. She didn't have all the pieces.

I've never lied to you and I won't start now. Never

lied. She'd believed that even when nothing else made sense. But if that was true ——

He wouldn't talk about it.

He said he wouldn't lie to her, but why couldn't he tell the truth, whatever that was? Who could he be protecting? Who —— ?

She spun into motion. Her handbag. Her shoes.

She called the doorman on the intercom.

A taxi. Right away.

She stood in the foyer waiting impatiently, then ran outside when the yellow taxi pulled up. She gave the driver the address of Allan's townhouse and the ten minutes' driving seemed forever but finally she was on the stairs, ringing her brother's bell. He didn't answer, but she had seen his car at the kerb and she pounded on the door until he came.

'What the hell?' Allan was wearing evening clothes with his tie missing. 'Do you have any idea what time it is?' He looked behind her. 'Jonathan? Where's Jonathan?'

She shook her head impatiently. 'We have to talk, Allan. Let me in.'

'Hell of a time of night,' he muttered.

'You weren't asleep. You're still dressed. Let me in.'

'Oh, hell.' He shrugged and opened the door fully. 'Come on, then. I was the same place as you. I saw you and Jonathan dancing but then you disappeared. We left early, too.'

She followed him into his sitting-room. He was limping heavily. 'We?' she asked. 'Who were you with?'

'Have a seat,' he said, not answering.

She walked restlessly to the darkened window.

'You look terrible,' he observed. 'Drink?'

'Mineral water.'

His brows went up but he went to his bar and mixed

a drink for himself and mineral water for her. 'This isn't a good time for a visit.'

He had company. A woman. Not here in the living-room. In his bedroom, she supposed. The accident fourteen years ago hadn't done much to tame Allan's wild ways.

She studied him as he limped towards her with the glass of mineral water. You couldn't count on truth when you were dealing with Allan. She loved her brother but she didn't trust him very far.

Trust. Jonathan. . .

He handed her the glass. She stared from the floating ice to her brother's face. He looked uneasy. She wondered if she had a hope of prising anything out of him, wondered if her growing suspicion could be true and whether she'd ever understand why the past was the way it had been.

'Jonathan and I aren't getting on very well right now,' she said. She looked up at him and he was drinking from his glass. She wondered if encouraging Allan to have a couple of drinks would make him more or less likely to talk.

'He offered me a job,' said Allan. He didn't meet her eyes.

'Jonathan offered *you* a job?'

'Yeah, well——' Allan laughed wryly. 'He said it was time I did some honest work. Let's call it a six-month trial.'

'You're actually *doing* it? Going to work for Jonathan?'

He shrugged and drained the rest of the glass. 'I leave for Vancouver first of the month.' He looked at her with a mask of innocence in his eyes and she knew she wasn't going to learn much. 'What's wrong between you and Jonathan?' he asked.

'He won't tell me what happened the day you two

were in that car crash.' She put her glass down on a coaster. 'Or afterwards. Things — things changed that day. Everything—— He won't talk about it.'

'You've heard it all before,' he said but something flickered in his eyes before he turned away to the bar and busied himself mixing another drink. 'What the hell would you want with details?'

She picked up her empty glass and followed him to the bar. 'I need to know why Jonathan won't talk about it.' She could see that Allan's tension was rising as she got closer. He wasn't going to tell her. She'd grown up with him and he'd run her ragged financially over the last few years. He'd also been the friend and confidant of her youth. She knew his ways as well as she knew Jonathan's.

He was hiding something.

She put the glass down on the counter.

'You aren't going to tell me either, are you?'

He dropped an ice cube into his glass. 'There was a car crash,' he said. 'You know that.' His hands were trembling. He lifted the glass to his lips and drank deeply. 'I got my leg smashed up. What else do you need to know?'

It had been a stupid idea, coming here. It wouldn't change anything. She couldn't force the truth from Allan.

Jonathan's voice echoed in her mind. 'Don't throw us away.'

'That's it, then?' she said. 'That's all there is?'

'What else did you figure?' Allan lifted his glass again.

Watching her brother evade her eyes, she realised that, even if she didn't understand the past, she'd come to trust the man she had married.

Jonathan had some hold over Allan. Neither of them was ever going to tell her what it was. He'd talked to

Allan and offered him a job and somehow he'd done something that had actually made Allan accept, although honest work wasn't her brother's usual pattern. And now Allan was turning his glass and looking innocent, but she knew him. Underneath the innocence he was afraid of her questions.

'Don't imagine you fool me,' she said quietly. 'It's taken me years to realise it, but that day — you were standing in the driveway with the keys in your hand. I saw you.'

Allan's hand jerked. 'You saw?'

'Yes.' The scence flashed again. 'Jonathan and Dad were shouting and you were standing beside my car with the keys.' She shouldn't have run away. If she'd stayed she would have seen what came next. 'The car hit a tree,' she said. 'That doesn't sound like Jonathan's driving.'

Allan wasn't listening and he wasn't watching.

'It doesn't matter,' she said, and she realised as she spoke that it was true. She wanted to know but there were other things that mattered more. The clock on Allan's mantel said it was five in the morning. Her gaze caught on the telephone.

Was Jonathan's jet still in the airport? Was he sleeping on the jet or in a hotel somewhere in Toronto? Or had he told his pilot to take off, to fly him away from her?

If he'd taken a hotel room she could find him in twenty minutes on the phone. She knew his taste in hotels.

'Cyn —'

'What?' she asked, but her mind was on the telephone and how she might use it to track Jonathan down. What difference if she didn't search out the details of what had happened? She could guess some of it. Jonathan must have protected Allan. She didn't understand why, but——

That scene on the porch——

She shuddered at the old pain but somehow she would learn to let it go. Something had happened that day that had torn apart their relationship for years, but unless she was completely mad all the evidence said that Jonathan loved her *now*.

He was right. They had to leave the past. 'Don't throw us away', he'd said, and she was a fool if she did because there would never be another Jonathan in her life.

If she could only find him. . .

When he'd left her at the condo he'd had a look on his face as if he was letting her go forever. But it wasn't going to be that way. She wouldn't let it happen. She walked stiffly towards the telephone. The satin trousers she'd been wearing ever since she dressed to go out with Jonathan were too tight. She must have put on weight since she last wore them. Soon she would put on more weight and her clothes wouldn't fit at all. She wondered how Jonathan would feel about the child they'd made. The child that she'd been told wasn't likely to happen for her. She hadn't told Jonathan. She'd wanted to solve the old mysteries first, to clear away all the shadows. But none of this mattered enough to risk what they meant to each other.

Jonathan. . .

He'd said he wasn't hung up on paternity, but he'd also said they could adopt, which she hoped meant he would be happy about the baby. He'd put that clause in the contract about if she had a child. So he'd thought about it and he hadn't planned to do anything to prevent it happening. And if she had been too stupid for too long. . .if Jonathan wouldn't listen to her when she finally found him—if he thought it was over now she'd find some way to prove him wrong.

She would tell him she was turning the tables on him. He'd trapped her with that crazy contract and if she had learned anything about him in these last few weeks it was that he'd had only one objective: to win her as his wife.

A real marriage.

So if she turned the tables on him and said there was a baby he'd have to stay still long enough to let her make him understand that she loved him. That she trusted him. That he still loved her, because everything he'd said and done in these last few weeks made sense only if he did love her.

A man didn't stop loving a woman in the space of a few reckless words thrown between them. A man didn't stop loving a woman in the space of a day. She drew in a deep breath and hoped that was true.

Whatever his reason for sending her away, all the evidence said that he'd never stopped loving her.

She reached for the telephone book and, behind her, Allan finally spoke.

'Jonathan said he'd burn that promissory note if I did six months' honest work for him.'

'That's exactly what Jonathan would say.' She flipped open the telephone book. He'd probably already burned Allan's note. It would be like him. Tearing up contracts. Burning promissory notes.

She ran her finger down the column of numbers. Which of these damned numbers would you call to find out if a private plane had taken off some time in the night? Had he gone back to Vancouver? She closed her eyes and prayed without words.

Jonathan. Please.

Allan said, 'Cyn——' and she shook her head. She'd heard enough of his denials. She'd spent her life worrying and watching him get in and out of messes and she knew he'd lied to her tonight.

'When I asked Jonathan to bail you out I asked him if he didn't feel he owed you something. He said he didn't owe you a damned thing.' She should have listened harder to what Jonathan *hadn't* said. She should have known, should have trusted him.

She reached for the receiver and the telephone rang as she did. She picked it up. 'Allan Dyson-Paige's residence,' she said mechanically. She'd fly to him if he was in Vancouver. She'd——

'Cynthia?'

She closed her eyes and felt the air drain out of her lungs. Jonathan's voice. 'Yes,' she whispered.

'Are you ready to come home?' he asked.

Her fingers locked tightly on the receiver. 'Yes. Will you—can you come for me?'

'Ten minutes,' he said. 'Wait for me.'

She hung up slowly. His voice had given nothing away. There wasn't anything to guess from those few words except that he hadn't left Toronto. And he'd been looking for her.

Jonathan was coming for her.

'Cyn?'

She had ten minutes to plan what she could say to erase the last three weeks. To erase all those words and put love in their place. Ten minutes.

'I was driving,' Allan said.

She dropped the receiver into its cradle. Ten minutes, and surely if he was willing to come for her. . . surely he would listen. 'You what?' she asked mechanically.

'I was driving your car when it crashed. Not Jonathan.'

She stared at Allan. She'd known. Of course

Jonathan hadn't driven into a tree. 'Why?' she asked. 'Why the lies? Why the fiction?'

'I thought he'd tell you,' said Allan. 'I figured when you said you were getting married—I called him right after you called me. I bloody well begged him not to tell you because—I don't know.' He still had the glass in his hand but it was empty again. 'I thought you wouldn't forgive me. Whatever deal they made I know it separated the two of you. You always were hung up on Jonathan and that was fouled up by—— So I begged him not to show you that statement. He said he wouldn't.'

There was a settee beside the telephone and she sank down onto it. 'What deal?' she asked. 'What statement?' She closed her eyes and tried to imagine the details. 'What happened, Allan? You had the keys. Jonathan was arguing with Dad. You—*you* drove away with Jonathan?'

'Yeah.' He limped to the window. 'I was just going to get into the car when they erupted on to the stairs and Dad was shouting. I'd already had a fight with Dad and I was going to take your damned car and keep going. I'd had enough. Then Jonathan and Dad on the stairs—Jonathan shouting that he'd take Dad apart one piece at a time if he ever hurt you again. That if you had so much as a bruise from horseback-riding Jonathan would damned well be keeping track.' He made a wild gesture. 'I thought they were going to kill each other, except that even in a rage Jonathan had that frightening control.'

Allan twisted his head to look at her. 'I'd have bet on Jonathan if it had come to blows, but I'm not sure it would have solved anything unless you were leaving town with him right after.'

'He asked me to,' she whispered. 'I was scared. If Dad caught us——'

'Yeah.' Allan had had reason enough to know that their father didn't take rebellion lightly. 'They both looked at me and I had the keys in my hand. I'd pinched the keys out of your purse. I knew I was in trouble anyway, so I got in and started the engine and Jonathan said something to Dad and he was coming down the stairs.' He shrugged. 'I called out to him. Want a ride? I said. He got in. I took off fast because Dad was coming down the stairs after me. I don't think Jonathan even knew I was there. He stared through the windshield and I was watching him and wondering what would have happened if he'd actually hit Dad. I heard him mutter that he wasn't letting that bastard hurt you again. I got that much, but he wasn't talking to me. Then I hit the damned tree and if Jonathan hadn't dragged me out of that car I'd have gone up in smoke when the fuel tank blew.'

'Jonathan. . .' She closed her eyes. She should have known that it wasn't Jonathan behind the wheel. But why couldn't Jonathan have told her?

It made about as much sense as the Greek alphabet. Jonathan had risked his life to save Allan from the accident. Then he'd taken the blame for the accident from everyone except maybe Alicia who hated Cynthia.

'Jonathan doesn't owe me a damned thing,' said Allan, 'but I owe him my life. I blanked out while he was getting me out of the car. I didn't wake up until the recovery-room after the surgery in the hospital. Dad was in there.'

'I don't understand,' said Cynthia.

Allan tossed his straight hair back. 'Dad always did like breaking rules although we never could, so it figures he'd get into the recovery-room. The first thing I heard was him growling that I was a stupid bastard and I'd better not forget who was driving.'

She moved a hand impatiently. Jonathan was coming. She wanted to be outside, to meet him outside.

'I'd have gone to gaol if I was the one behind that wheel. No licence and those other charges of impaired driving on my record. And I was old enough to be tried as an adult, was old enough when Dad bought me out of the last jam before that.' He shrugged. 'So Dad told me Jonathan was driving and I'd better not forget it. I didn't argue.'

'Jonathan kept you out of gaol?' She shook her head. 'But why would he do that?'

'They made some sort of deal.' He gestured towards his damaged leg. 'I guess while they were both in the waiting-room and I was under the knife. Jonathan has my confession, my statement that I was driving. That was part of the deal. The nurse witnessed my signature and Jonathan took the statement. I remember him looking at Dad with that paper in his hand and saying, "I'll be watching and I *will* use this if I have to."'

Jonathan was coming for her. Coming to pick her up. Even though she hadn't trusted him enough he wasn't giving up on her.

'Cynthia. . .'

'I'm going to wait for Jonathan outside,' she said. She would search the street, anything to make him come faster. Jonathan hadn't done it for Allan. He'd made a deal with her father and she understood it all now. Not the details, but she understood *why*.

Allan paced unevenly across the room towards her. 'I guess I won't be seeing much of you now?'

She touched his arm. 'I do understand,' she said. 'Dad terrorised us. Of course you were afraid to go against him.'

Allan evaded her eyes. 'Do you think Jonathan still has that confession?'

She thought Jonathan would have burned it, but, if

so, that was Jonathan's to tell. 'Ask him,' she suggested.

She moved towards the door. Ten minutes, he'd said, and how many gone now? Five perhaps. She wished she'd changed because the satin trouser-suit was wrinkled and Jonathan was coming for her.

'Say hello to your friend,' she said. 'The woman in the bedroom.'

'Oh, lord! I forgot! She——'

'Thank you, Allan.' She reached up and kissed him and then she ran outside because maybe it had been ten minutes.

Jonathan. . .

The street was empty. Quiet and artificially lit. She went down the stairs slowly because she was wearing high-heels and she wasn't taking a chance of falling. Test positive, the doctor had said. What would Jonathan say to that? First she had to tell him that she loved him and that she would follow him to the ends of the earth. She grinned at that because, knowing Jonathan, they could well end up at the end of the earth. Perhaps he'd be building a palace in some exotic country next? Or a world-peace centre in Europe? Or——?

Wherever he went, she was going to be at his side. He'd married her and he was stuck with her now. If only he still cared. . .still felt what he'd felt when he'd smiled into her eyes and——

Her hair!

She fumbled with it and shoved the clasp and the pins into her purse. Then she rummaged for a comb in her handbag just as a car turned the corner ahead.

A white limousine.

Jonathan!

She started running. The limo stopped and the door opened and she froze because Jonathan was getting out

and suddenly she wasn't confident at all. She was
terrified.

She stood on the pavement as he got out and they
were perhaps four feet apart, staring at each other. He
gestured into the limo. She nodded mutely and he held
the door as she climbed in and sat down. Her legs were
trembling. He sat beside her, but not touching. The
door closed and then she felt the car start to move.

'We have to talk,' he said. His voice was harsh in the
muted silence of the limo. 'I can't take much more.'

'It's over,' she said.

'No,' he said. 'No,' and his face had turned grey and
bleak.

'No! Oh, Jonathan! Not that! I mean I——' She
gulped and touched his shoulder and felt the jerk of his
reaction. Then his arms went around her and she was
trapped tight against him. She closed her arms tightly
around his neck so that his face was buried against her
hair. 'I'm not running anymore,' she promised raggedly. 'I—I can't—you——'

The rest of the words tangled up in her throat.
Mutely she turned and sought his mouth with hers and
felt a deep shudder go through him. She sighed against
his mouth and let her body settle into his. When he
pulled her across his lap she curled up against him and
laid her hand along the side of his face. As he moved
his mouth against hers she could feel the flexing of his
muscles, an erotic feedback that left her breathless.

He drew back. Silence, and the red echo of muted
light on plush upholstery. Jonathan's eyes dark and
studying her. His arm supporting her back. His hand
on her breast. She felt a shudder of desire as he
breathed in and his body moved against hers. The
strain in his face was gone now, and his eyes were dark
with fire.

'Where are we?' she whispered. She touched his face.

'I don't know.' His fingers tangled in her hair and he bent down towards her. Her lips parted and lifted to meet his. She felt his breath drain out. 'I told the driver to find somewhere quiet and not to disturb us.' His mouth sought hers and she threaded her hands through his wild dark curls and pulled herself tight against him so that every beat of her heart was echoed in him.

'Good,' she whispered. Her hand slid down along his chest. He was still wearing evening clothes and she frowned at the barrier of his jacket.

'I intended to keep you here in the back of this limo until we settled things.' His hand slid along the satin of her buttoned jacket. 'We have to talk,' he said again.

She found the buttons of his shirt and managed to unfasten the top two. Her voice sounded breathy and she hoped it was seductive. 'Later. We can talk later.'

His hand covered hers. 'Will there be a later?'

'Yes.'

She heard the quick intake of his breath, but he growled, 'Not here. When we make love——'

'Hold me,' she begged.

'I'm not letting go. Don't you understand that yet?'

She sighed and rested her face against his chest.

'You're tired.' His voice rumbled in his chest.

'I've been tired a lot.' She struggled to sit and he shifted to let her so that she was facing him in the faint light. 'First I—Allan told me he was driving when my car crashed.'

His hand stilled. 'He said what?'

'That he was driving. That you saved his life.'

He shook his head. 'That's a long time back.'

'He said he begged you not to tell me.'

'Yeah.' He touched her face gently. 'When we got married. And, like a fool, I agreed. At the time I

thought it wouldn't matter. That we could start again.'
He touched her face and said soberly, 'I didn't realise
how much it mattered to you. If I'd known——' He
shook his head. 'That morning—when I said I wouldn't
wait for you——' He shuddered, and his voice went
harsh. 'I knew I'd lose you forever in that instant but
I'd promised your father I'd get out of your life. I
didn't want to hurt you. That's the last thing I wanted.
But it was the only way.'

'You took the blame for that accident to buy my
safety. You made a deal with Dad that I'd go to
Switzerland if——' She gestured vaguely.

'Not Switzerland. Anywhere that you weren't under
his roof. It was the only way I could protect you. But I
had to promise to keep away from you. And I tried to,
but——'

She touched his shoulder and felt the tremor of his
response. 'Don't stay away,' she said. 'Don't ever stay
away again.'

His voice deepened. 'When you came asking for
money I knew it was a gamble but I had to try to win
you. I'd spent years of hell knowing you belonged to
another man. You were free and you'd come to me—I
knew damned well by then that I wasn't going to forget
you.

She cradled his face between her hands and said
intensely, 'The more I thought about it, the more it
didn't make sense that you were driving. That's why I
went to Allan's tonight. I thought—but I couldn't
understand why you'd let yourself be blamed if Allan
was at the wheel. The only thing was—I realised that
you'd never once actually said to me that you were
driving.'

She felt his jaw moving against her hands as he
spoke. 'I couldn't lie to you.'

'That's why I went to Allan, because I finally under-

stood that if you wouldn't lie and you wouldn't tell
me—it meant you *couldn't* tell the truth. And Allan
had to have the key to that.' She breathed in his scent
and realised that the tension in her stomach was gone.
Jonathan's arms were around her and his voice was
filled with emotion. 'Allan wasn't going to tell me
anything,' she said, 'but I realised I was being a fool. I
was reaching for the phone to start trying to find you
when you called. It was afterwards that Allan told me
the truth. There's no reason for you to believe me
but—even if Allan hadn't confessed I was coming
looking for you.'

He covered her mouth with his and said in a low,
husky voice that trembled, 'I love you, moon lady. I
always have.'

'I dreamed you saying those words.' She breathed in
his love and threaded her fingers up into his hair. 'I
was prepared to trap you if I had to. Until you learned
to love me again. . .because I told myself you had to
love me even though you'd never said——'

'Never said?' He was astounded. 'How could you
not know?'

'Oh, Jonathan. . .' She laughed and slid her hand
down over the buttons of his shirt. 'I've loved you
always. . .I—— Can we go home to bed?' she whispered. 'Now?'

He shuddered and his hand slid under her jacket and
found the silk of her bra. She saw his throat spasm.
'These doors lock,' he said. 'It's very private back here.
Tinted windows. Privacy. . .'

She felt a delicious wave of sensual excitement
tearing through her.

'But you're very tired,' he murmured. The buttons
to her satin jacket slipped apart under his urging and
he pushed the fabric back over one shoulder. She saw
him swallow. 'Maybe too tired?'

'Not that tired,' she whispered. She pushed his jacket back on his shoulders. His pulse beat heavily as their hands fumbled. When her jacket was a pool of satin on the floor of the limousine he went very still. He reached out with one hand and traced the lacy line of her bra.

'You are so beautiful,' he whispered.

She unfastened the last button of his shirt and pushed it back so that she could run her hands over the planes of his chest. 'I like the way you look, too,' she whispered. 'I love you. . .dream of you. . .the way you feel. . .'

He drew her down so that they were kneeling on the carpeted floor of the limousine. He ran his hands lightly down her arms. She shivered and he drew her closer.

'Inside me,' she breathed. 'I dream of how you feel inside me.'

'You said you would trap me. . .' His eyes were molten shadows a heartbeat away from her. 'I can't imagine running from you but. . .' His lips brushed hers and she whimpered as he slid the strap of her bra down over her shoulder. 'Trap me,' he urged. 'I want to be trapped by you.'

'We're going to have a baby,' she said huskily. For a moment it was as if he didn't understand her. Then she felt the tremor go through him.

'Are you sure? You said—you said you couldn't.'

She rested against him, felt the strength of his arms and the warmth of joy growing inside her. 'One chance in a thousand, they said, and I guess—I always knew you could work miracles. I——' Her laughter was suddenly nervous. 'Jonathan? You don't mind, do you?'

'You know the answer,' he growled, and of course she had known. He crushed her against him. 'My wife. . .our child.' His hand smoothed the riot of her hair. 'I'm going to make love to you,' he said in a deepening voice. 'I really meant to wait,' he vowed. 'To get you to a real bed where we had all the time in the world. . .to love you as you've never been loved before. I wanted forever with you, to show you——'

She stretched her arms around his shoulders and whispered, 'Make love to me, my darling. Please. . . now. . .'

'I never could resist you,' he admitted roughly. 'You are the most incredible woman. I don't know how I've lived all these years without you.' He ran his hands along her body and drew her gently into his arms. 'Now, moon lady. . .love me. . .let me love you.'

He took away the last of the barriers between them and she sighed in pleasure as she showed him how she would love him through all their life together.

HARLEQUIN ✦ PRESENTS®

HARLEQUIN PRESENTS
men you won't be able to resist
falling in love with...

HARLEQUIN PRESENTS
women who have feelings
just like your own...

HARLEQUIN PRESENTS
powerful passion in
exotic international settings...

HARLEQUIN PRESENTS
intense, dramatic stories that will keep you
turning to the very last page...

HARLEQUIN PRESENTS
The world's bestselling romance series!

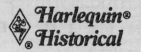

Harlequin® Historical

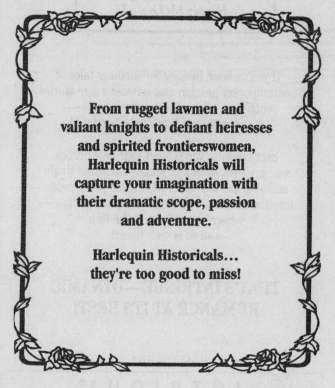

From rugged lawmen and
valiant knights to defiant heiresses
and spirited frontierswomen,
Harlequin Historicals will
capture your imagination with
their dramatic scope, passion
and adventure.

Harlequin Historicals…
they're too good to miss!

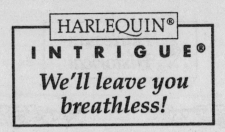